L     **DATE DUE**

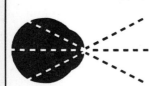

# LAW ON THE FLYING U

## B. M. BOWER
### Edited by Kate Baird Anderson

**WHEELER PUBLISHING**
*A part of Gale, Cengage Learning*

GALE
CENGAGE Learning·

Detroit • New York • San Francisco • New Haven, Conn • Waterville, Maine • London

## GALE
### CENGAGE Learning·

**LIBRARY OF CONGRESS CATALOGING-IN-PUBLICATION DATA**

Bower, B. M., 1874–1940.
    Law on the Flying U : western stories / by B.M. Bower ; edited by Kate
Baird Anderson. — Large print ed.
        p. cm. — (Wheeler Publishing large print Western)
    ISBN 978-1-4104-4987-0 (softcover) — ISBN 1-4104-4987-4 (softcover)
    1. Ranch life—Fiction. 2. Montana—Social life and customs—Fiction.
3. Large type books. I. Anderson, Kate Baird. II. Title.
PS3503.O8193A6 2012
813'.52—dc23                                             2012018171

Published in 2012 by arrangement with Golden West Literary Agency.

Printed in the United States of America
    1  2  3  4  5      16 15 14 13 12

FD202

# PERMISSIONS

# TABLE OF CONTENTS

# FOREWORD

The short novel, "Chip of the Flying U", in the October, 1904 issue of *The Popular Magazine* kicked off Bertha Muzzy Bower's career, and anchored a long series featuring Chip Bennett and the "Happy Family". These stories were based on real ranches and real people in and around the tiny, remote cow town of Big Sandy, Montana. The Flying U saga continued through dozens of short stories, fifteen hard cover books, and a number of silent and sound films. Bower's friend, Charlie Russell, illustrated her first book, G.W. Dillingham's hard cover version of *Chip* issued in April 1906, as well as *The Range Dwellers* in 1907, *The Lure of the Dim Trails* in 1912, and *The Uphill Climb,* published by Little, Brown & Company in 1913. Over the years Bower (the name my family called her at her request) wrote just as realistically about other Western locales.

From 1903, when she sold her first story to a classy magazine while living near Big Sandy, to 1940, the year she died, she also lived and gathered story material in California, Idaho, Nevada, Arizona, and Oregon. That personal knowledge was vital to her writing style and growing success in the demanding Western literary market. Bower produced sixty-five hard cover books from *Chip* to *The Family Failing,* published posthumously by Little, Brown & Company in 1941. That was a remarkable accomplishment for anyone, let alone a woman who started as a Minnesota-born housewife with only an eighth grade rural education.

Her parents, Washington Muzzy and Eunice Miner Muzzy, were not typical of their humble social class as hard-working pioneers, homesteaders, and farmers. Mr. Muzzy was also a musician and builder who became a leader of the Minnesota Farmer's Alliance, and had many articles and letters published on political economy, a hot topic in that era of runaway capitalism, booming national expansion, and successive financial depressions. Mrs. Muzzy had earned an Illinois Teacher's Normal School certificate, and was teaching in Wisconsin when she and Washington met. Both were unusually intelligent and resourceful, lovers of good literature and music, politically progressive Republicans, as well as Abolitionists, teetotalers, and devout Northern Baptists with high moral standards, all passed on to their youngest daughter.

To compensate for Bertha's lack of higher education, Washington Muzzy encouraged her to read widely and sharpen her powers of observation. The unusual regime of self-education coupled with her curiosity and interest in progressive ideas and subjects made her more knowledgeable than most women of her era. She loved to read and quote the Bible. A quiet supporter of women's rights, she was also in favor of strong unions for workers and farmers, birth control, and other controversial issues, all of which found their way into her work. The popular and sacred music the Muzzys and then the Bower family enjoyed at informal home gatherings also appeared in her stories. She was an excellent cook; food sometimes provided major story elements.

While Bower lived in northern Montana, she paid close attention to the land and people, particularly the stories ranchers, cowboys and others told her about their lives, giving her a treasure trove of story material. From 1903 on, mentor Charles MacLean, editor of *The Popular Magazine,* gave her a hand up from the publishing end. She also enlisted a talented cowpuncher, William Brown "Bill" Sinclair, as range consultant. He provided the main inspiration for Chip Bennett — including his taciturn nature, and odd habit of tearing a strip from his cigarette paper before adding the tobacco. She earned enough to escape her abusive marriage in 1904, then married Bill, who was also writing successfully under the pen name Bertrand W. Sinclair. The fledgling authors had no qualifications for the profession beyond uncommon mental powers, love of literature and word craft, and intimate knowledge of a profitable pulp fiction subject — the last remnant of the real Wild West in its final years.

From that difficult beginning, Bower became the first woman to make a living writing Western fiction, and in my opinion was the most prolific and creative. She met publishing deadlines on time, and proved to even the most critical readers she "knew her stuff". Sharp, ironic humor, crisp, authentic but clean dialogue, believable characters, and a fine sense of place were her other secrets of success.

But few fans ever learned that their favorite author was in real life an attractive, feminine divorcée with wavy auburn hair, creamy skin, warm hazel eyes, good legs, and grace and poise in every inch of her five feet of height. To protect her growing market, her publishers cautioned her to keep the secret. They believed readers would reject the work of a woman, especially a divorcée. Thus her personal story was largely a mystery until the 1970s when popular culture became a legitimate field of academic study. Even then, few authorities acknowledged the value of her contribution to the Western genre. Judge for yourself. Here are nine tales from her first three decades of writing.

Bud Cowan, another Big Sandy cowboy, once told her of the trouble his outfit had after they fed a stray Canadian steer, inspiring "The Intervention of Almighty Voice" in which the Flying U outfit is plunged into similar difficulties. Most people around Big Sandy knew of the outlaw and whiskey trails from Canada down through the Bear Paw Mountains and Missouri River badlands (they're still in use, by the way), and the ranches where Butch Cassidy, Kid Curry, and their kind found sanctuary. Bower made the perils of the lawless life painfully clear in "The Outlaw". She must have known an irritating windbag like "Big Medicine", who offends the entire Happy

Family — but she allowed him redemption, which she often did miscreants. In "The Land Shark" she portrayed another familiar type in homestead days, the deceitful, greedy real estate agent, with biting irony. One of her best novels, *The Flying U Strikes* (1934), features a slightly more honest woman agent. In the 1933 "Law on the Flying U", Bower gave broader treatment to an earlier theme, the close bond between a man and an unusual horse. She loved driving as well as horseback riding and, as her income improved, owned a succession of sturdy autos. "On the Middle Guard" featured a "goggle-eyed" automobile, one of the first on the range, as the starring character. At the end of a long series of Flying U short stories in 1912, Bower chose a California *vaquero* she had known as the model for "The Native Son", who brings out all the Happy Family's resentment and prejudices against pretentious outsiders. Another Flying U regular, slow, humorless Happy Jack, the natural object of many jokes, becomes "Happy Jack, Wild Man" through an accident every range rider fears. Bower may have been reflecting on her failed marriage to Bill Sinclair when she wrote "By Gollies, Yes" in 1919 about the hazards and benefits of close partnership, and the loyalty and determination required to make it last.

*Break Your Own Trail,* the title Bower chose for the life story she could not write herself, is coming together based on personal material and records my mother preserved, and my own extensive research. I have also spent time in Montana, especially in and around Big Sandy where I met descendants of Bower's character models, and recognized many story settings. Much of the land looks the same, although grain is now the main crop instead of beef and horses. Big Sandy Creek still runs narrow, clear, and cold on its crooked way north from the Bearpaws to the Milk River. The Log Cabin Saloon that furnished the model for Rusty Brown's place is now a combination café, bar, and bowling alley — and other original buildings are still in use. Take my word for it — B.M. Bower's West is still very much alive.

Kate Baird Anderson

# THE INTERVENTION OF
## ALMIGHTY VOICE

Happy Jack slammed the stable door shut and fastened it, and then turned to gaze moodily after the Old Man, who was riding across the frozen creek on his way to a neighboring ranch.

"I tell yuh, I don't like the way things is going," he complained to Cal. "Trouble's sure headed this way on the jump."

"Yeah . . . it generally is, according to you," Cal assented. "What particular brand uh trouble have yuh spotted now?"

"Matrimony," said Happy Jack mournfully.

"Nobody don't call that trouble, till a year or two after it happens," Cal retorted. "It's blue-joint to the eyebrows, and clear spring water gurgling in every coulée beforehand." Cal swung open the big gate and whistled cheerfully.

"Aw, gwan. Must be you're stuck on having that old parrot of a Kohloff woman bossing the hull ranch. I guess you don't know her as well as I do."

Cal turned his face away from the searching north wind, which they were bracing their bodies against. "It's too blame chilly out here to argue the point!" he cried over this shoulder, and trotted up the hill to the bunkhouse.

"Shut the door!" chorused four strong-lunged voices when he entered.

"Happy's just behind," he informed them, and sought the comfort of the stove. It was good to be in the warm little cabin again after a long ride in the cold. The air was heavy with cigarette smoke, and sultry with heat from the big coal stove.

"How's the mercury?" Jack Bates inquired.

"I never looked. She ain't no kind uh weather for a picnic, I tell you those. The Old Man's plumb welcome to his ride over the hill."

"That's what he done," put in Happy Jack. "Gone off with his nickel-plated shoes and that little dinky overcoat with the velvet collar . . . and a han'ke'chief tied on under his hat . . . his stiff hat. And in a north wind that'd shave the hair off a yaller dog!"

"He's sure got it bad, these days," Cal remarked commiseratingly.

"He'd ought to be close-herded in a home fer the feeble-minded," Slim declared.

"You needn't say anything, Slim," Chip remarked caustically. "I can remember a time when you had all the same symptoms . . . and for mighty near as slight cause."

Slim snorted profane words, and emptied the coal hod into the stove.

"If it was for some nice girl now, a fellow could overlook a lot uh foolishness," mused Jack Bates. "But when yuh think uh that old catamount he's playing up to. . . ."

"He'll be her third, if she gets him," Chip said. "And it's a cinch she'll get him if she wants him . . . she's that kind."

"It's his dough she's after," grumbled Slim. "She don't care nothing about *him*. She wants to get her clutches on this here Flying U layout . . . which I will say is temptin' to 'most anybody."

"D'yuh know," Cal spoke up, hugging the stove so closely that his clothes began to smoke, "I'd kinda like to see the Old Man get some nice woman that'd think a lot uh him, and . . . and all that. He don't have no uproarious good time, I reckon, holding down the White House all by his little lonesome. I'd like to see him setting out on the porch of a summer evening, with some nice woman beside him, and flowers in the windows . . . and a kid or two, maybe. . . ."

"The Widder Kohloff has got five," Jack Bates observed reflectively.

"Bah! I never meant that old skate. She . . . oh, damn!"

"Same here," muttered Chip, glancing up from a picture he was drawing on the bottom of a cigar box.

"Say, ain't it 'most time to let the mourners pass out?" Weary wanted to know. "The Old Man ain't married yet, and the Widow Kohloff ain't giving us our orders every morning before breakfast, either. Cheer up. How far did you and Happy escort Almighty Voice this time? Didn't beat yuh home, did he?"

"We worked a new scheme on him today . . . hazed him clear down to Denson's," said Cal. "It's a kinda mean trick to play on a neighbor, maybe, but we thought it would interest 'em to hear Almighty run the scale a few nights."

"It ain't right for us to play the hog and keep all the concerts to ourselves," added Happy Jack, contorting his features into what passed for a smile.

"It wouldn't hurt Bill to take a few lessons from him," commented Chip.

Cal laughed. Bill Denson's singing was a

standing joke in the neighborhood. "They could put up a swell duet if they'd just practice up a while."

"By golly, ole Almighty Voice don't need no practice," Slim declared earnestly.

"I'd tell a man he don't," Chip agreed. "The way he's been training his voice out here in the creekbed every night for a month, I guess he's graduated in music."

"Did yuh hear him knock the top off high G last night about midnight?" asked Weary.

The others groaned assent.

"Well, we can maybe get caught up on sleep, now," Cal boasted comfortably. "I'll bet he don't sing under our lattice, love, for one while. Eight miles won't look good to him."

"I guess nobody'll lay awake nights crying for the sound of his voice." When Chip said that, he voiced the sentiments of the Happy Family to a man.

In the last three weeks Almighty Voice had become an important factor in Flying U affairs. When he first drifted into the coulée in the midst of a bitter three-day blizzard, the boys took pity on the great, gaunt, wistful-eyed stray, and threw a generous fork full of hay over the corral fence to him. Before the sky cleared and the snow swirl was lulled to rest in the bright sunshine, many forks full of hay had followed the first, and the big steer took to waiting for his ration with as complacent an assurance as was exhibited by any animal bearing the Flying U brand on its ribs. A week had not passed till the boys repented of their charity, but the wistful-eyed stray was undismayed by the hardening of their hearts against him.

Whether the sun shone or the blizzard raged, he must eat if he would live. And blue-joint hay, cast down in a fragrant heap before his eager nose, was a luxury unknown since his calfhood. Three days of such bounty had taught him to regard with contempt the short buffalo grass that must be sought with much patient gleaning back on the wind-swept range land. No more would he nose in the snow for his dinner; a mistaken kindness had spoiled him. When he was fed, he ate greedily; when he was not fed, he stood stubbornly close to the corral fence and bawled unremittingly the day through, and the night.

The Happy Family noted the Canadian brand on his lean ribs, marked the depth and volume of his plaint, and forthwith named him Almighty Voice, in dishonor of a notorious renegade Cree. In two weeks, the boys took for granted the daily ceremony of driving Almighty Voice up the grade and far back on the hills. Almighty Voice, wise beyond his kind, quickly learned what was expected of him and trotted amiably away from the ranch, placidly secure in the knowledge that his exile would be brief.

At first the Happy Family rode out in a bunch and assailed him by weight of numbers and terror-breeding language. But the ranch work must be done, and forcing 900 hungry calves to wait for their dinner while five fretful cowpunchers argue with one Canadian stray is not fair. Soon the boys paired off and took turns.

Thus it was that Almighty Voice returned each night to bellow behind the bunkhouse, and two wrathful young men saddled their horses each morning to escort him back to the range. Weary said that the ranch wouldn't seem like home if some night Almighty Voice failed to return and charge wakefully through the bushes along the creek, and bawl the long, dark hours away — but the others refused to argue with him, and Weary himself was palpably insincere.

"The Old Man said this morning not to give Almighty another spear uh hay . . . not if he bellers the underpinning out uh the sky," Shorty told them when they went to supper that night.

Cal, thinking how neatly he and Happy Jack had solved the problem, grinned sarcastically. "The Old Man's a little out uh date with them orders," he fleered. "From now on it's up to Denson to give him the marble heart . . . or else adopt him.

Almighty Voice, scenting the three great haystacks in Denson's corral, trotted with long strides down the frozen trail that led into the coulée, and straight to the stable yard. He was weary from his eight-mile journey — and as to his appetite, he was chronically hungry. He crowded close to the fence and sniffed longingly through the rails.

Bill Denson, coming out of the house just then, caught sight of the big red stray, and whistled three short, commanding calls. Almighty Voice heard and glanced abstractedly over his shoulder, and turned again to his sniffing. Further along, a rail sagged, leaving a wide space, and he made for the place, tentatively thrust in one long, finely curved horn, then the other.

When Bill arrived, Almighty Voice was in the hay corral to his shoulders, and straining every muscle to go farther. His great pink tongue stretched eagerly out and grasped a luscious mouthful. Then the dogs — two yellow curs — nipped viciously at

26

his heels and recalled him to his weary fight against circumstances. He would have turned tail instantly had he been free, but his horns caught against the rails and his great untaught heart was seized with a panic of fright. He twisted and jerked blindly, and broke a rail square off.

Two minutes later, Almighty Voice was disappearing into the sunset on the trail that held his downcoming hoof prints, and Bill Denson was whistling off the two yelping yellow dogs that still yapped at the red steer's heels.

At ten o'clock the Old Man put his head into the bunkhouse door. "Why didn't some uh you boys chase that stray offen the ranch?" he roared into the somnolent darkness. "I just drove him out uh the hay corral and tied the gate . . . it was left open by *somebody.* I want some uh you fellows to make it your business to haze him out onto the hills first thing in the morning. He'll eat his dog-goned head off before spring. I won't have it. I got cattle enough uh my own to feed, without feeding all the dog-goned strays in. . . ." The Old Man slammed the door just then, and went on up the hill to the house, saying things into the little turned-up velvet collar of his coat. Evidently his temper was not at its sweetest — which was not strange if one considered the figure where the mercury stood, and the inadequate clothing of James G. Whitmore.

When the sounds of his muttering had died away, Chip Bennett rolled over and uncovered his head. "It's sure a mean trick to play on a neighbor," he remarked at the stove, which yawned redly at him in the dark.

"No more singing under our lattice, love, this winter," came a voice one might safely guess was Weary's.

"Yes! Why the dickens didn't some uh you fellows chase that stray off the ranch? What are yuh drawing wages for, anyhow?" queried Jack Bates in the Old Man's querulous tones.

"Aw, go to 'ell," Cal told them all savagely.

Outside, the frozen willows down by the creek rattled ominously, and a plaintive, deep-throated *m-bawh-h-h!* wailed, long-drawn in the silence — a foretaste of what was to follow.

Next morning, Jack Bates and Slim climbed into their saddles in vengeful mood and, swinging the loops of their ropes threateningly, started Almighty Voice up the grade on the run, while the Old Man watched grimly from the stable.

Toward sundown a wind crept down from the northland, and with it came the snow falling, fine and thick, and stinging sharply the cheeks that faced it. With it also came Almighty Voice — tired, hungrier than ever, and clamoring at the injustice of man.

"Poor old devil," said Weary apologetically to Chip. "He ain't to blame because hay looks good to him on a night like this. Maybe we'd raise a howl ourselves if we was as cold an' empty as he is."

"I'd tell a man!" responded Chip. "I'd give him a hand-out just to keep his courage up, if the Old Man hadn't said. . . ."

"That's all right. But d'you suppose the Old Man'd miss a fork uh hay . . . or a ton? Almighty Voice could live like a king, right here in the corral, and the Old Man'd never feel it. I never go against orders . . . but still, a night like this it's plumb wicked. . . ."

"You know yourself, Weary, it'd only make him harder to get rid of. He'd bawl worse than ever, if he got any encouragement," argued Chip. "And he's big and husky, and able to rustle like he's always done. He's range-bred from the ground up. Don't you ever think he don't know how to nose his supper out of the snow."

"Oh, all right," said Weary reluctantly. "Of course, what the Old Man says is bound to go. But that steer'd chew his cud peaceful tonight, if I owned the Flying U brand."

"I wish you did, Weary."

Weary turned and threw a snowball unerringly at Almighty Voice, shivering tail to the storm just outside the corral where the hospital bunch was feeding luxuriously upon sweet-smelling blue-joint. Then Weary fastened the gate securely and followed Chip up to supper, turning deaf ears to the stray's plea for charity. But when the boys left the table and adjourned in a body to the bunkhouse, Weary was not among them. He was speeding surreptitiously down the hill to the corral — and such was his celerity that he was back before he was missed. Even Chip failed to notice his absence.

An hour later, when the rest of the boys were deep in a game of seven-up, Chip, listening to the cruel beat of the blizzard without, felt his heart grow soft within him, caught up his cap and mittens, and moved unobtrusively to the door. The boys, wrangling over who played "low" — which both Weary and Happy Jack claimed with much obstinacy and argument — took no heed of his going.

Just before bedtime, James G. Whitmore himself opened the door of the White House to look out upon the weather, and was beaten back by the storm that half smothered him. He spluttered, brushed the snow out of his eyes, and shut the door with unnecessary force. He thanked the Lord his beasts were well housed and full stomached. Then his conscience mentioned a poor, half-starved stray standing, supperless, without his gates, and he wriggled uncomfortably in his big Morris chair. After a minute he muttered something about being too dog-goned soft-hearted to live, and, bundled to the eyes, fared fretfully forth into the storm.

Next morning when the boys went down to feed the stock, they found Almighty Voice calmly chewing his cud, lying in the snuggest corner of the corral shed along with the hospital bunch. And just over the fence lay two generous little heaps of snow-shrouded hay, the stray wisps of it blowing an unheeded invitation in the wind.

"Well, I'll be damned!" said Shorty when he saw the telltale heaps, and he drove Almighty Voice, with much vituperation, out into the open. But the Old Man, coming up behind, coughed hypocritically into his fleece-lined buckskin mitten, and said never a word.

James G. Whitmore was not a lady's man;

on the contrary, he had rather shunned than sought the feminine portion of Choteau County's population, content to live his life as he would, his heart given wholly to the care of the Flying U Ranch and the Flying U cattle, and to the joys and sorrows of his Happy Family.

He was easy-going and indulgent, and, if he waxed querulous at times — when his rheumatic leg was misbehaving — and stormed at the boys upon slight provocation, the Happy Family shrugged its square shoulders and told itself philosophically that the Old Man's leg must be acting up again. They thought a great deal of the Old Man, did the Happy Family.

How it ever came about that he began to consider the Widow Kohloff from a matrimonial viewpoint, James G. Whitmore himself would have found it impossible to explain. Perhaps the guileful widow could have done it. The tactics of her campaign were extremely simple, but nonetheless effective for that — because, as I have said, the Old Man was not accustomed to the wiles of women.

She began by asking James G. Whitmore's advice upon certain business matters — she who boasted that she was sharper than any man that the Lord had ever made — and she flattered him delicately by acting upon his advice, thus showing faith in his judgment. A man likes to be considered shrewd; the man or woman who so considers him rises immediately in his estimation. James G. Whitmore began to think the Widow Kohloff a pretty smart woman.

She bought the cattle he advised her to buy. Incidentally she needed someone to advise her upon the management of the little herd of a dozen head. Also incidentally she never failed to set before James G. Whitmore some practical demonstration of her expert cookery and the general excellence of her housekeeping.

James G. Whitmore had all a cat's love for a cozy corner in a warm room, and he loved crisp, freshly fried doughnuts, and coffee that had a shine in its rich clearness when it was being poured into his cup. The Widow Kohloff could be very nice, when she liked. Once, when the Old Man called upon her to see how the cattle were coming on, and to inquire if they showed any symptoms of scab, she discovered a certain hoarseness in his voice, and gave him some delectable hot drink, and coddled him as he had not been coddled for more years than he liked to count.

That night when he was alone in the White

House, he looked around him with a dissatisfied air. When he went down to supper, he found fault with Patsy's coffee, and called it slop. He wanted to know why in thunder Patsy couldn't make doughnuts that a man could eat without having to take the axe to them first. He said Patsy's pie crust wasn't fit for coyote bait — which was rank injustice. Everyone knew that Patsy's pies were things to long for; one need only watch the Happy Family dispose of a half dozen blueberry pies to be convinced of that.

Patsy slammed the kettles around on the stove till the noise he made carried far into the night, and he muttered weird things in German that the Old Man could not understand. James G. Whitmore pushed back his chair with a peculiarly rasping sound, and went off to sulk through the evening.

The Happy Family scented danger for the Old Man that night, and swore about the snare set for his unaccustomed feet. Happy Jack, who had worked for the departed Mr. Kohloff and more fully realized the doom that threatened them, sorrowed more keenly than did the others.

"You mark my words," he said lugubriously, "two weeks after the wedding'll see your finish. In the first place, she's religious,

34

an' she won't allow no cards on the ranch . . . and how's a fellow goin' to put in these long evenings without cards? Besides, she's p'nurious as the devil. She'll dock our wages for every minute we ain't tearin' the bone out workin'. Didn't I get docked quarter days every time it rained, or anything? She had me counted right down to the hours . . . and, if yuh happen to be a minute behind time . . . oh, gee! She'll just about take your head off. Bein' late is the unpard'nable sin, according to her."

Seems to me," put in Weary mildly, "you're kinda overlooking the Old Man."

"Old Man be darned!" Jack retorted bitterly. "I ain't overlookin' him any more'n what she will, once't she's got her noose on him. The Old Man won't cut no lemons, except when there's checks to sign . . . and she'll take mighty good care he ain't overworked in that line."

All the discussion in the world, it seemed, could not save James G. Whitmore. Each night saw him more thoroughly dissatisfied with bachelorhood. Each morning he awoke to a greater distaste for Patsy's cooking. Whether he was in love, James G. Whitmore had no means of knowing, for no precedent had existed in his life; besides, he shrank from speculating upon the subject. He was not the man to sit down calmly and ask his heart leading questions.

He knew that the windows of the White House were dingy from need of washing, and that the windows of the Widow Kohloff's house shone beautifully clean. He knew that the rooms of the White House were, somehow, dreadfully cluttered with things not built or intended for ornament, and which more properly belonged farther down the hill — and yet the rooms seemed bare and cheerless. No amount of heat — and he had the stove red to the rim most evenings — could make the parlor as cozy as was the parlor of the Widow Kohloff.

James G. Whitmore, heretofore content to smoke his pipe in solitude and the depths of his big Morris chair, had awakened to the fact that his Eden wanted its Eve. Whether with the coming of Eve, he might inadvertently admit the serpent, he did not consider. And there was no getting around the fact — Patsy's coffee never had a shine to it when it was being poured into the cups!

Black gloom settled upon the Happy Family when it was known beyond all doubt — Shorty told them — that the widow had "won out", and the Old Man was going to get married.

Things could never be the same with the

Old Man married to a shrew like the Widow Kohloff. Happy Jack, remembering the biting sharpness of her tongue, took mournful pleasure in contemplating the black future. Once he wondered aloud where they would all be two months from then — but Chip told him shortly to "close his face", and Happy Jack did so, comprehending all at once how sore a subject it was.

He was not the only one of them who wondered where they would all be. Once away from the Flying U, they would inevitably scatter, and the Happy Family as a unit would be only something to remember, and to smile wistfully over on night guard when the stars set one to thinking; to tell tales of to new comrades; to hunger for in troubled times as one hungers for the days of barefooted boyhood.

Although they never dreamed it, the Old Man himself lay often awake wondering how it had happened, and half tempted to wish it had not happened at all. The Widow Kohloff as an angler was ingratiatingly amiable and dependent; as a fiancée, she showed symptoms of wanting to dictate in matters which did not properly concern her — and James G. Whitmore had a temperamental aversion to any interference in his business affairs. He was puzzled and uneasy over the change. Still, they were certainly engaged, and the Old Man never went back on a bargain.

Came a day when the license to marry was properly recorded in Great Falls. On Sunday, an itinerant Methodist minister would preach in the Meeker schoolhouse, and he had agreed to drive over to the Kohloff Ranch immediately after, to officiate at the wedding.

That Sunday is one which the Happy Family will tell of to their sons — if sons there ever be.

All night the north wind had wailed around the corners of the bunkhouse; all night had Almighty Voice bellowed distressfully along his hard-beaten path in the creekbed.

Not a man in the Flying U coulée had slept soundly, for various reasons. Not a man but rose that Sunday morning unrefreshed and truculent. Even Weary Davidson was in a villainous temper — a state of mind without precedent in the Happy Family.

The Old Man stormed at Patsy because the coffee was bitter and the hot cakes heavy — although, in truth, the heaviness was all in the Old Man's heart — and flounced out, if a man may be said to flounce, leaving his breakfast half eaten. Patsy grumbled in throaty German, and the Unhappy Family glowered at their plates. For want of a better scapegoat, they vented their wrath upon Almighty Voice as the most tangible grievance at hand.

"I'll bet money he won't keep everybody on the ranch awake again," declared Jack Bates, after five minutes of promiscuous vilifying.

"Going to drive him down to Denson's?" taunted Chip.

"Dickens of a lot uh good that would do," snapped Jack, in no mood for banter. "I move we tin-can the old devil. We ought to 'a' done it long ago."

"Canning goes," said Weary recklessly. "We'll celebrate the great day proper." And that was the nearest anyone came to mentioning the real cause of their ill-humor.

The day was cloudy and cold. The wind had changed to the southwest, and blew chill and damp — that unpleasant stage of a Chinook when its nose is yet cold from its combat with the frost.

The Unhappy Family scattered to its morning work. There was hay to haul and spread for the 900 calves; there were the horses to tend, and the stables to clean, and the hospital bunch to feed. But after that was done, it being the Sabbath, they might spend the day as they chose.

Till dinner time they worked moodily, saying little. After dinner they trooped up to the bunkhouse, and Jack Bates reverted to their quarrel with Almighty Voice.

"Come on and can the old tramp," he urged. "He'll hang around till Kingdom Come if we don't."

"It's going to Chinook," remarked Cal. "I guess he can make out on buffalo grass from now till spring."

"Well, let's get busy then," said Weary, drawing his cap down over his ears.

"Where's Almighty at?" Slim inquired, feeling under his bunk for his overshoes. "I ain't seen him for a couple uh hours."

"Aw, he ain't run off . . . you needn't worry," said Happy Jack. "I seen him in the old calf shed a while ago. He's catching up on sleep, so's he can deal us misery again t'night. I'm onto him bigger'n a wolf."

They went to the storehouse and unearthed an old copper wash boiler, and adjourned to the stables.

Shorty hailed them from the mess house door. "Hitch up the creams," he yelled, "and tie 'em to the fence! The Old Man's due to start in half an hour."

Chip and Weary went to get the team ready, and never had they obeyed an order more unwillingly. By the time the rig was ready and the horses tied to a corner of the fence with their heads to the road, a commotion over behind the stable by the big corral told them that the boys had not wasted any time. They hurried to the place.

Almighty Voice had knowledge of the pinch of a noose, and fought warily. He was fairly caught with Jack's rope around his wide spreading horns, but he had no thought of surrender.

Slim threw and missed. Slim never was much good with a rope, but he failed to realize his shortcomings; according to his version, his failures were the result of bad luck.

"Here, let me get hold there!" cried Chip authoritatively, and Slim coiled his rope and climbed down, complaining because the wind was too strong and the rope too light. Something always did ail Slim's rope.

Chip swung into the saddle and rode close, widening the loop to his liking, whirled it twice over his head, and flipped it from him with a deft turn of his wrist. The wide loop dipped and snared the unwilling feet of Almighty Voice, the wily, the indignant. Chip jerked up the slack, and the rawhide hissed around the saddle horn when he took his turns. Almighty Voice went down with a hoarse bellow that promised things yet to come. His great pink tongue lolled angrily; his eyes turned glassy with rage.

Stretched helplessly in the snow between two good lariats manipulated by skillful hands, he bided his time. Weary and Happy Jack made fast the boiler to his tail by one of its handles, took off the head rope, and retreated to the corral fence where Slim was already perched like an exceedingly plump, overgrown partridge.

Almighty Voice kicked himself free and got up to take note of his surroundings. He had not felt the searing iron, which surprised him much. The flinging of ropes had heretofore been but the prelude to much physical discomfort. He shook himself, wondering at the total absence of any ill effects. He eyed the boiler dispiritedly and turned to walk away. The boiler rattled behind him. He stopped, regarded it with more interest, and turned to snuff investigatively. The boiler turned, also, which was strange.

He took a few tentative steps, eyeing the thing over his shoulder; the boiler followed. Almighty Voice stood still and considered. He was a steer that hated mysteries; he had found many in his four years of range life, and he had never yet left a problem until it was solved to his satisfaction. He threw up his head and stared resentfully at the men who had thus affronted him. They laughed, and someone threw a clod of frozen snow; it struck him fairly in the ribs, and he jumped. The boiler jumped, also.

Almighty Voice kicked at the thing and it mocked him brazenly. He stopped, tossed his head, then lowered it and made straight for Jack Bates. Jack's horse dodged and scudded out of sight around the corral. Then Jack, not caring to take any risk, shut his horse into the safety of the corral and went and perched on the top rail beside Weary.

Almighty Voice whirled and charged again, and the corral gate speedily closed upon Chip's mount, and Chip roosted with the others on the fence. Thus cheated of his revenge, Almighty Voice busied himself with tossing clouds of loose snow belligerently over his back and rumbling, deep in his lungs, his "war talk". After that he beat emphatic tattoo upon the boiler, which resounded in deafening volume.

Patsy, hearing the uproar and guessing what was the matter, went down to see the fun. He did not see much of it, for he had no sooner appeared than he was rushed, and he made all haste back to the mess house where he was justified in feeling safe. Almighty Voice shrouded himself in a snow veil and bellowed triumph.

"He don't stampede worth a cent," remarked Weary, wrinkling his cold-stiffened cheeks into a smile.

"I'll tell a man he don't!" responded Chip. "He's all for making rough-house around here. Look out! He's going to take a header at the fence!"

Almighty Voice struck the fence like a ram, and came near dislodging Slim, who was rolling a cigarette and was never known to have his mind on two things at once. The steer backed off for another try, and then bethought him of new devilment. He raced around the stable, the boiler at his heels, and in just thirty-one seconds the creams were flying across the creek with lines trailing. The Happy Family sat on the fence and gasped, while Almighty Voice stood back and surveyed them judicially.

"Say! It's up to somebody to get a move on and stop those horses," began Chip, "before. . . ."

"Who in thunder let that team get away?" roared a voice that could be heard a mile away. "What's going on here, anyway, I'd like to know?" Presently the Old Man knew. He was out in the open when he first comprehended the situation, and the nearest shelter was the old calf shed. For a man nearing his fifties and troubled with rheumatism, James G. Whitmore gained the roof of the shed with astonishing celerity. Almighty Voice raged futilely just below him, and sent dirty, unbeautiful snow up into his face. The Old Man scrambled back from the hail of it and cried: "Sic 'em, Tige! Sic . . . sic . . . *sic!*" — which was at best only a pitiful bluff. There was not a dog on the Flying U Ranch, and never had been. Moreover, Almighty Voice, being a range-bred steer, knew nothing about dogs, or about the sounds best calculated to insure their presence.

"Why in thunder don't yuh do something?" the Old Man yelled to the Happy Family. "Yuh set there in a row like a lot uh dog-goned snow birds. Git your horses and drive this —" insert adjectives here to suit the occasion — "steer off. Are yuh *glued* to that dog-gone rail?"

The Happy Family descended to the inner side of the fence and got their horses. Cowboys, like soldiers, are wont to obey orders. They rode out and did the best they could, which was to keep out of the way of the long, tapering horns of Almighty Voice.

James G. Whitmore, perched uneasily upon the calf shed, watched the performance and stormed unavailingly. Shorty and Slim, on the trail of the vanished creams and the buggy, had sneaked down the creekbed and so gained the grade. Meanwhile the wind blew chill, sweeping up the coulée at a fifty-mile gait — and James G. Whitmore was clothed to please the eye rather than for comfort. Also, time was passing.

He looked at his watch and groaned. It was fourteen minutes past one, and he was to be married promptly at two o'clock; the preacher had an evening appointment at Dry Lake, and the preacher lived for his preaching. A mere wedding ceremony would not tempt him to delay in the saving of souls — that the Old Man knew.

Whether the Happy Family really did their best, none can say. They certainly managed to give a splendid imitation of a real Spanish bull fight — barring the costumes and the matador. Also, the audience, limited though it was in number, grew terribly excited before it was over, so much so, in fact, that the Old Man came near falling through the shed roof, which was rotten with age.

James G. Whitmore's watch told him it was twenty-five minutes past two, and his body was chilled to the bone when finally the end came in this wise.

Almighty Voice had long since kicked the bottom out of the boiler, and the tough copper sides, made in one long piece, loosened at the rivets and flew out straight. When Almighty Voice kicked again, an end flew up and whacked him unexpectedly on the rump. He bellowed, a new note of terror in his voice, and rage was submerged in a sudden panic. Straight across the creek and up the grade he went like an ungainly red comet, and disappeared over the hill in a swirl of snow.

James G. Whitmore climbed stiffly down and rubbed his rheumatic leg. "I want to see every dog-goned one uh you fellows up at the house in the morning," he snorted. "I'll have something to say about this here p'formance. You can be packing your war bags between now and then." He gave another despairing glance at his watch, and went, in deep dejection, up to the mess house to thaw out.

By the time the creams had been rounded up and the cracked buggy pole wound temporarily with baling wire, another hour was spoiled. James G. Whitmore, uneasy but conscience clear, drove away to his belated wedding. On the way he rehearsed many times the exact wording of his explanation, which he instinctively felt required much finesse to save it from being wholly ridiculous.

And the Unhappy Family meditated gloomily in the bunkhouse, with consciences not entirely clear, while they gathered up their belongings and packed their war bags as they had been ordered to do.

In two hours James G. Whitmore was back again, and he came alone. In view of the fact that it was nine miles to the Kohloff Ranch, it was obvious that he had not stayed there long. The boys put up the team and returned to their mediations — and their packing.

Happy Jack, for once knowing whereof he spoke, wanted to bet that the widow had roasted the Old Man aplenty for being late, but no one had the spirit to take him up. Shorty, sorry and helpless, moped with the rest of them. He was not so sure but he would be fired with the rest.

James G. Whitmore, his ears burning with the biting sharpness of the widow's tongue, looked about him that night with a sigh of pure thankfulness. The room, cluttered with many things not made for ornament, and which more properly belonged farther down the hill, seemed to him the coziest, most soul-satisfying place in the world. He thought of what might have been if the widow had not lost her temper so completely, and he shivered.

His rheumatic leg ached frightfully, in spite of the Three-H liniment he had been vigorously applying for half an hour — but James G. Whitmore owned himself happy. He rubbed his leg absently, and grinned. Later, when warmth and much friction had eased somewhat the pain, he leaned back and filled his pipe luxuriously, still smiling. He was thanking the Lord his Eden was unequivocally Eveless, and likely to remain so. Searching his pocket for a match, he drew out a legal-looking paper and eyed it with aversion. It was the license. He read it slowly through, grunted, and twisted it into a long, thin tube, opened the door of the stove, and deliberately thrust it among the glowing coals — then as deliberately withdrew it and lighted his pipe. After that, he settled down upon the small of his back and smoked contentedly.

An hour later, just when the Unhappy Family was preparing for bed, the Old Man opened the bunkhouse door and put his head in.

"Say," he began in a tone elaborately casual, "if that dog-goned stray shows up here again. . . ."

"He won't," interrupted Weary, the irrepressible. "Most likely the King's riders have nabbed him by now for smuggling. There's probably a duty on copper."

The Old Man grinned appreciatively. "Well, if he does show up," he said, "turn him into the corral and give him the best there is till grass starts. And, say! A couple uh you better take a look at the lower fence t'morrow. I met Bill Denson, and he says there's a dozen of our calves down to their place."

He slammed the door, and the Happy Family looked at one another and drew a long, relieved breath.

# THE OUTLAW

In the beginning of it, Lee Allan was not much out of the common, just a big, wire-muscled, carefree cowboy, with much skill in the taming of broncos, and with always a certain reckless light deep down in his hazel eyes — if only one knew enough to look for it. But there was nothing particularly reckless in his behavior, for all that. He rode and shot better than most men, and when he gambled, he did not often lose. He was not given to brawling. Men liked him and knew him for a "square" man.

Then quite unexpectedly, he fell in love. Always before, women had been mere pleasant incidents which were not worth much worry or loss of sleep, so that just at first Lee didn't quite know what ailed him. With him, to love at all was to love much, and foolishly to place the woman high up on a pedestal and do homage as a man sometimes does believing that he has found the unfindable — a human being with no faults whatever. This is all very uplifting — until that disastrous time when comes disillusionment, then it is a toss-up whether the lesson is going to prove a blessing or a curse.

Lee Allan loved the girl as wholeheartedly as a man can — and for a time he held her fancy and was happy. He was straight and tall and good to look upon, and the reckless flicker just back of his eyes piqued her interest a bit. She liked to look into them and speculate upon the real man of him, and to feel that she held complete mastery over his life. It flatters a girl to know that a man has stopped gambling for her sake, and that he is living soberly and virtuously simply because of her.

She even went so far as to think seriously of marrying him, and to give him a promise — with those mental reservations that play the mischief, sometimes. Lee, taking her at her word and not knowing anything about her mental amendments, naturally thought the matter was settled and was filled with great content. He began to think of a homestead and a little bunch of cattle taken on shares

Then someone told him to look out for Dick Ridgeman, the banker's arrogant, sneering, spoiled son, and hinted at complications that might arise in Lee Allan's plans. Lee went straight to the girl, who did not deny it. Her promise had been false, but he blamed his rival for sweet-talking her into the lie. He started out blindly to find Dick Ridgeman.

He found him, all right — his match so far as size and strength were concerned. Lee was just a primitive young man at heart, and he thought he was fighting for his own. They went at it savagely with clenched teeth and muscles strung tautly for combat. They fought with bare fists, fairly, with the weaker due to get soundly thrashed. A crowd gathered in the street to watch, so there were plenty of witnesses when the two finally flung apart and stood for an instant free of each other. Then Dick Ridgeman reached back with his right hand. His gun was half out of its holster when Lee drew his own gun and fired — he was the best shot in the country, and the fastest. The accomplishment cost him dearly.

His first thought when Dick Ridgeman fell was to go and tell Alice what had happened. Time enough after that to give himself up — or to pull out, he did not quite know which.

The girl seemed frightened and horrified when he told her, but she clung to him, and begged him to wait. He must have a cup of coffee before he started on his long ride, and she would get him a lunch in case he must ride farther and faster than he thought. If he loved her, she said, he would let her do that much for him.

Lee waited, and considered whether it were worth while running away at all; still, it was nice to be petted and waited upon, even if he had been unlucky enough to shoot a man. It showed that the girl really cared for him, after all. And to Lee that overtopped everything just then; he had so lately been almost convinced that she did not care.

While he was waiting, determined to tell her that he would not run, the sheriff walked in and arrested him. Lee had forgotten that the sheriff lived just around the corner — but it really made no difference, since he meant to surrender anyway. So he comforted the girl, and told her not to worry about him — he'd come out all right.

But he didn't. At the trial — and because it was the banker's son he had killed, the trial came very soon — he had his first real shock. The girl appeared as a witness for the prosecution.

Lee didn't quite understand at first. When she told the jury that she had been engaged to Dick Ridgeman, Lee stared at her incredulously. When she admitted — under question, it is true — that Lee had threatened to "fix Dick Ridgeman so he wouldn't bother anybody," he caught his breath. It was true, and not true. He remembered telling her that he would fix Ridgeman so he wouldn't want to bother *her* for a while, which was not quite the same. But when it came out that she herself had sent word to the sheriff that he was with her, something went wrong in the heart of Lee Allan, and the world became full of a great, unnamable bitterness.

For all that, he sat quite still, and the reporter only transcribed that **the prisoner winced perceptibly once or twice when Miss Alice Thomas was giving her testimony, but otherwise he appeared quite unmoved.** When a man received the cruelest blow of his life, it speaks well for his fortitude if he only winces once or twice.

Even if they had given him justice — but they did not. He had killed the son of the Honorable John R. Ridgeman, the great man of Colton, and Lee Allan was just a well-meaning, hot-tempered, daredevil cowpuncher. They gave him ninety-nine years — convicting him of murder — and told him how fortunate he was, and how lenient were they that he was not to be hanged.

That night Lee twisted two bars in his cell window and escaped, leaving a characteristically brief and comprehensive note behind:

**Damn the law and the lawyers! It's all a rotten fake — and your jail ain't much better. It's me to the wild bunch.**

**Lee Allan**

To the "wild bunch" he certainly went, but only figuratively speaking. He remained a solitary fugitive. The first reward for his capture was only a paltry $1,000 — because they did not yet know their man. When a posse, after riding far and fast on his trail, turned back and suddenly found themselves ambushed in a narrow gully, and emerged from the trap with every man of them painfully but not permanently crippled — Lee was certainly an artist with a gun — the reward jumped to $5,000 and the fugitive became a man of importance in the county.

A month later when the sheriff and his deputy met Lee face to face in the badlands, and the badly frightened deputy brought the sheriff back with a bullet hole in the fleshy part of his right arm, the law awoke to the fact it had a bad man to deal with, a very bad man, for whose body, dead or alive, $5,000 was not considered too high a price. The Honorable John R. Ridgeman doubled the amount, so that Lee Allan was worth just $10,000 to the man who succeeded in capturing him.

After that he became alternately the hunted and the hunter. He must have had friends who stood by him — cowboys are a clannish lot — for he never seemed to lack ammunition. His rifle was remarkably accurate at long range as more than one enterprising outlaw-hunter could testify, exhibiting on return the corroborative evidence of bullet holes in non-vital parts. More than that, Lee seemed always abreast of the news, and undoubtedly knew of the large reward.

For some months the badlands witnessed a desultory war at long range, and always with the same result. Men who regarded covetously the $10,000 went boldly out to slay and spare not. Without exception, they returned more or less painfully wounded and one or two were brought back to the coroner.

Lee Allan persisted in remaining distressingly alive, and in a year he had that part of the badlands practically to himself. It began to look very much as if the $10,000 must go begging indefinitely.

Two sheriffs had been disposed of, and the third was laughed at when he told his constituents that he would capture Lee Allan or be killed by him. He was two months in office, and had been kept very busy overhauling a gang of horse thieves, so that the public waited curiously and a bit impatiently for the grand encounter, and speculated much upon the result. In the meantime, Lee Allan was left with not a soul to shoot at, which must have been wearisome to the last degree.

Colton was not what one might call a large or important town, and, except during shipping seasons and when court was in session, it dozed beside the river with nothing much to justify its existence. At certain times it was insufferably dull, which is the way of cow towns in midsummer.

It was at such an hour that the Honorable John R. Ridgeman stood quite alone behind the cashier's wicket in his bank, for the bank was quite as small and unimportant as the town, and there was little business transacted that day. The Honorable John often took the cashier's place for an hour or so at lunchtime. He was doing some aimless figuring upon a blotter when a stranger opened the door and walked in composedly, bringing with him an indefinable atmosphere of the rangeland.

At the first glance, the Honorable John passed him over casually as some small cattle owner, perhaps wanting a loan. At the second glance, his mouth half opened and his face became the color of stale dough. He reached out nervously for a revolver that lay always conveniently near, but the stranger laughed unpleasantly. The Honorable John drew back his hand and stared at him.

"I hear you've had a reward out for Lee Allan for quite a spell now," began the fellow. "And you stand good for half. Ten thousand dollars for him, dead or alive . . . that right?"

The Honorable John ran the tip of a nervous tongue along his dry lips, which even then refused him speech. He answered with a queer convulsive little nod.

"Yuh had it up a long time . . . seems too bad yuh ain't had a chance to pay it out to some enterprising varmint. I've brought your man in . . . and he's just about as alive as he can be. Cough up that ten thousand, old-timer. Yuh won't have another chance . . . not in a thousand years."

The Honorable John "coughed up". That is, he began shoving bundles of bank notes under the wicket, till Lee Allan stopped him impatiently.

"No, thank yuh. I'll take the gold."

"Eh . . . excuse me," mumbled the Honorable John quite humbly for so great a man, and went for the gold — but not alone. Lee Allan very calmly went with him to the vault, carrying his gun ready for instant use in his right hand. The Honorable John fairly trotted, so great was his anxiety to get that $10,000.

$10,000 in gold is rather heavy — heavier, perhaps, than Lee had expected, although he did not say as much. He lifted the bags, slipped them into a larger one that he took from his pocket, and smiled whimsically. The Honorable John could see nothing funny about it, for he was still facing the gun and all that it suggested; he still wore the stale-dough complexion, and his manner was ill at ease.

"It's lucky yuh didn't make the offer twenty thousand." Lee grinned. "I'd 'a' had to make two trips after it . . . and by the looks, your nerves wouldn't stand for another visit, old-timer. Yuh needn't be scared. Yuh ought to be glad to see me, the way you've been mourning around over my absence. Do I look good to yuh ten thousand dollars' worth? Well, so long. Yuh likely won't meet me again for some time. This'll last a while . . . rent's cheap down in the badlands, and a man don't blow much money there."

He had tied the loose top of the bag into a hard knot, working deftly with his left hand. Now he pushed the Honorable John R. Ridgeman into the vault, closed the door, and walked out of the bank as calmly as he had entered.

Outside, he walked quietly down a side street toward the river where he had left a boat drawn up on the bank. He had slipped his revolver inside his trousers band, and the bag of gold he carried upon his left shoulder. Figuratively he looked the whole world in the face, for he made not the slightest attempt at concealment.

A saloonkeeper, standing outside his empty saloon, saw Lee disappear around a corner, and stared incredulously. Surely it was nothing more than a remarkable resemblance, he thought — although it would be hard to mistake that tall, straight-limbed figure or the proud set of the head. He stood looking at the corner and wondering if his eyes had tricked him.

Aside from that, no one saw Lee except a woman who came to the door of her shack to throw out a pan of water. Lee passed within fifty feet of her, and she stopped and stared as the saloonkeeper had done. Lee looked up and smiled at her astonishment. Inwardly he said: *Lord what a pair of feet!* The woman's feet were large, but one would scarcely expect an outlaw, who had just claimed and received the reward upon his own head, to notice a woman's feet.

On the riverbank half a dozen children were playing around the boat. "Here! Yuh better pile out uh that, kids," he commanded, but gently. They stood back and eyed him curiously while he placed the bag in the boat and thrust an oar into the soft clay bank. He was positive that the oldest boy recognized him, but he did not hurry. When the boat floated clear, he sat down and adjusted the oars, looked up at the staring group, and held the oars poised in air.

"Say, kids!" he called. "Yuh better run home and tell your dads that the Honorable John R. Ridgeman is shut up in his bank vault, and I don't believe it's any too well ventilated. Hike along before he uses up what air there is. And, say, tell that little tin sheriff uh yours that I'll leave him a note in this boat. Get a hustle on, now!"

The sheriff was not in town, and it was two hours before he was notified; it was three before he reached the place where the boat was moored. Three hours would carry the outlaw far toward his hide-out in that jumble of barren hills that were the badlands, so the sheriff went about his investigation deliberately. Allan's message had been given him verbatim, and he looked first for the note. It was easily found, and his name, Bob Farrow, was scribbled upon the outside so there could be no mistake. Also, there was no mistaking the utter scorn of law in the few lines of the message, which was this:

**Come on down and play tag with me — if you ain't afraid. Bring a possy along so I can practice up shooting. If you come alone I won't shoot you. I'll just tie you to a tree and let you starve to death. You'll come a-running — I don't think!**

**Lee Allan**

Bob Farrow was not a coward. He straightened so suddenly that the boat rocked under him and little waves licked along the sides like gray tongues. He gritted his teeth and swore.

"I'll go . . . and I'll go alone. Thinks he can bluff me, does he? He'll eat this note . . . or I don't come back."

"What does he say?" queried an old fellow who had come up with the little crowd from his shack down by the ferry.

The sheriff, every tone vibrant with contempt, read the note aloud.

The old man had known Lee Allan long, and had liked him. "Better not tackle it alone, Bob," he said uneasily. "He'll git yuh sure as you're born . . . and he'll do just what he says, too."

"Would you take a dare like that?" demanded the sheriff angrily. "Anyway, what am I sheriff for?"

"Yuh ain't sheriff to commit suicide," said the old man calmly. "I voted for yuh, Bob, and I hate to see yuh tackle the job single-handed. Lee's desp'rate. He used to be as white a boy as you'd find . . . but he's got a price on his head . . . that'll change most anybody's temper, I reckon. Don't yuh go alone, Bob."

Farrow laughed shortly, read the note slowly through once more, and put it carefully away inside his memorandum book. "I'll go play tag with him all right," he said grimly, "and I won't come back alone . . . I promise yuh that."

He mounted his horse, meditating on the insult and how he should avenge it. The old man still stood on the edge of the bank, combing his rusty-red beard with his fingers and shaking his head ominously; the sheriff looked at him and laughed.

"Yuh mustn't be too blame' sure about Lee Allan winning out, old-timer!" he shouted a bit boastfully, and turned to discuss the hold-up with his friends.

Many warned him, and many begged to be taken along. But for every fresh applicant, his refusal was tinged with a deeper annoyance. Why should they be so sure of his failure? It was man against man, both well armed and able to hit what they shot at. He could not see where Allan would have any particular advantage, except that he was familiar with the battle ground. On the other hand, Allan had given his promise not to shoot the sheriff — which he would doubtless regret. Farrow smiled to himself; *he* had not handicapped himself by a promise of any sort; he would certainly shoot on sight.

He went about his preparations calmly in the face of much unheeded advice and remonstrance. To the men of Colton, the fact that any man was determined to go out alone to capture Lee Allan seemed proof that his mind was not right. They called him a fool privately, and wished him luck publicly, and let it go at that.

Next morning at sunrise the sheriff jogged down to the ferry with a well-laden pack pony ambling at the heels of his horse, and with a smile for the melancholy farewells of the early risers who he met. The old man came out of his little shack on the far riverbank and looked after him bodefully.

"See yuh later!" called the sheriff cheerfully, and laughed at the general air of gloom with which his levity was silently reproved.

Farrow looked back at the little town, sent a mute good bye to a certain girl who had cried the night before with her face hidden on his shoulder, and faced south calmly. He did not ride as though moments were very precious, for he was of the sort who can hold impatience in leash and hasten slowly. He had a grubstake that would last him two weeks — longer, if he were put to the necessity — and ammunition aplenty. With the town and the river behind him, his eye went appraisingly over his outfit with satisfaction.

He settled into his saddle contentedly, and slipped the reins between his fingers while he made a cigarette. Then he faced the rim of yellow-brown hills, and went on with the leisurely dog-trot that carries a man far between sun and sun, and does not fag his horse. And while he rode, that last jeering line of the note chanted over and over in his brain and fitted its taunting measure to the hoof beats of his horse — *"You'll come a-running — I don't think!* — till the words whipped his resentment into a cold rage that held no place for mercy.

At dusk he camped in the very edge of the badlands, and knew that the game began on the morrow, and that it was to be played out to the end — which was death if he lost. For the other, death or shackles, as fate might determine. But Bob was not afraid of the outcome. His dreams had nothing to do with outlaws and their haunts; they were all about the girl who had cried upon his shoulder.

When he swung again into the saddle, the sun was gilding all the hilltops, and the hollows were gloomy and chill with the night that had gone before. He felt keenly for the first time the magnitude of the task he had set himself. Somewhere in that bleak, barren jumble before him, Lee Allan lurked and waited for his coming — but where? The stony hillsides gave no trace to follow. It must be an aimless quest, with the finding left to chance.

The sheriff rode warily, choosing instinctively the easiest path and watching like an Indian for signs of life among the silent pinnacles, stopping often to examine with field glasses some far-off object that looked suspicious, and that turned out nothing more than blackened rock, grotesquely human in form.

At noon something whined past him and spatted against a rock ten feet in front of his horse. He pulled up sharply and listened; the far-off *crack* of a rifle echoed mockingly among the rocks. He turned and eyed the gaunt hills behind him, but they held their secret in grim, unsmiling silence. He swore aloud, got off his horse, and examined the rock that had been hit. He picked up a bit of flattened, steel-jacketed lead, and slipped it into his pocket. Then he looked again behind, searching with the glass the sheer walls of the bluff, mounted his horse, and went imperturbably on. The game, he told himself, had begun.

Just at sundown another bullet sang plaintively and flicked up the yellow dust in the cow trail he was following. He got off and hunted for it, found it, and put it with the other — and his fingers trembled slightly.

"I'll give him bullet for bullet . . . the cur!" he comforted himself. He did not try very hard to discover the source of the shot. The outlaw was evidently using smokeless powder, and there were more than a thousand places within long range that might be his hiding place. The rifle crack told nothing, for the hills caught up the sound and distorted it with their echoes, as if they were in league with the outlaw and took pleasure in throwing the sheriff off the scent.

That night he sat with his back against a rock wall with his rifle across his knees, and with eyes wide open and his ears strained to catch the slightest sound — of sliding gravel, or the click of boot heel upon rock. The stars rested their toes upon the jagged pinnacles and blinked down at the lonely black hollows that lay sleeping beneath.

All night he sat there watching, and at day's dawn boiled his coffee, fried his bacon, and ate his breakfast moodily. After that, he packed and saddled, and went on, heavy-eyed and savage with the world.

Half a mile, and a third bullet spatted significantly against a boulder ten feet from the trail. Unconsciously Farrow noticed that the bullets always struck approximately ten feet from him; even in missing him, Lee Allan showed accurate marksmanship. With teeth grinding, he got down and went after the bullet. A bit of paper, held in place upon the boulder by a stone, fluttered as if eager to claim his attention. He jerked it viciously loose, and read the laconic message:

## Tag! You're IT!

He shook his fist impotently at the sullen gray crags, and shouted curses that the rocks gave defiantly back to him, word for word. When he had calmed, he went on doggedly.

When the rock shadows were but narrow frills of shade came another leaden reminder that he was watched, and he knew now the song it sang: "Tag! You're *it!*"

He searched for the bullet anxiously, feeling Lee Allan's scornful dark eyes following his every move. When he had found the bullet and dropped it with the others, he ate his lunch feverishly and went on, doubling, turning unexpectedly north and south and west as he found opportunity, hoping to fool his enemy and throw him off the scent.

The sun was setting red when the fifth singing messenger hit ten feet before him. That night he sat as he had done the night before, with his back to a rock and the rifle across his knees, and waited and watched, and strained his ears for faint sound in the still, brooding silence of the wilderness.

That night there were no stars to keep watch with him; a cold wind crept down the rock-strewn gulches and chilled him as he sat, but he did not move; he did not dare. He only listened the harder, and peered into the black with eyes that ached with sleep hunger, and waited for the dawn.

Late that afternoon, when the bullets he had gathered numbered seven and when the strain upon nervous and physical endurance was too great to be borne any longer, he fancied that there was movement among the huddle of black, scarred boulders across the narrow gulch. He raised his rifle, and fired his first shot. Half a minute, perhaps, and dull-eyed, he watched the place.

"If I killed him," he muttered aloud, "I could sleep." It had come to that, then — he must sleep. Killing Lee Allan was after all but the clearing away of an obstacle to his sleep. He became unreasoning, malignant. His clouded brain, strained to the limit in those two days and nights, had place for but one idea — to kill.

He fired wildly at every rock, every stunted sagebrush that his distorted imagination could construe into the semblance of a man. He emptied the magazine of his gun, and refilled it feverishly, emptied it again, while the fantastic peaks and cliffs and hollows barked jeering reply. Save for the echoes, there was no sound, and he laughed gloatingly.

A bullet — the eighth — hummed close to his ear and kicked the dust under the very nose of his horse. It threw back its head nervously, and Bob, forgetting where he was and the precarious path he followed, jerked the reins savagely and dug deeply with his spurs. They went down together, sliding and rolling to the bottom of the gully. The horse struggled wildly, gained his feet, and stood with the saddle hanging upon one side, eyeing his master curiously. After a time he took a tentative step or two, shook himself disgustedly, and began nibbling the scanty grass growth. Up on the trail, the pack pony gazed into the gully and whinnied lonesomely.

When Bob opened his eyes, it was to see where all the water came from. His head and face were dripping, and the first conscious thought was met by another dash of water in his face.

"How the dickens did yuh fall over that bank?" a voice questioned plaintively. "Yuh wasn't shot . . . and neither was your horse." The last words were spoken defensively.

Bob raised to an elbow and stared grimly at the man. The cold water seemed to have cleared his brain. "Hell!" he said, and lay back again. There did not seem anything else to say.

"Yes and then some!" assented the other petulantly. "Do yuh know your leg is broke?"

"No matter," said Bob laconically. "I can starve just as long with a broken leg."

"You was a fool to come," complained Allan. Yuh might 'a' knowed you'd get the worst uh the deal."

Farrow looked at him. "I'm Valley County's little tin sheriff," he reminded, "and that ten thousand would come handy to start housekeeping with." He was holding himself steady with an effort. When he stopped speaking, his lips twitched with pain and weakness.

Allan stood irresolute, looking down on him with close-drawn brows. "Who . . . is she?" It was as if the words spoke themselves, against his will.

Farrow opened his eyes and looked at him squarely, challengingly. "Her name's . . . Alice Thomas," he said defiantly. "We was going to be married in six weeks."

He saw Allan wince, and closed his eyes, satisfied; if he had to die, he had at least

73

struck one blow home, he thought.

Allan sat down on a rock and rolled a cigarette with unsteady fingers. "I suppose," he said slowly, "yuh think a lot of her." He lit a match, held it to the cigarette, and took three puffs. "And yuh think she . . . likes you," he finished deliberately.

"I know it!" flashed Bob, forgetting for the moment his hurts, anxious only to wound the other.

Allan said nothing — but his cigarette went out many times before he finally threw it away. Bob sank into a stupor born of his great weariness, his hurt, and his loss of sleep. He was roused by a great wrenching pain, and struggled wildly.

"Lay still!" commanded the voice of Allan. "I just had it in place."

"What . . . ?"

"I'm trying to set your leg . . . if yuh'd keep your nerve. Can't yuh stand nothing, yuh lobster?"

Farrow lay still and clenched his teeth; he didn't like having even Allan think him a coward. When it was over, he was weak and giddy, and felt only vaguely that he was being moved, and that the new place was softer and more comfortable. After that all was blank.

He opened his eyes to the sun of another

day, and his nostrils to the smell of frying bacon. He discovered that he was lying between his own blankets — and with memory came wonder. He raised painfully to an elbow and discovered Allan sitting upon a rock beside a campfire, rolling a cigarette while he kept an eye upon the bacon frying in the sheriff's frying pan. Instinctively he reached toward his hip. Allan caught the movement — being an outlaw must breed wariness in a man — and he frowned.

"Better lay down," he said evenly. "I didn't think yuh was such a sneak . . . but I didn't take no chances. Yuh ain't got any more gun than a jack rabbit, old-timer."

"I'm not a sneak. We ain't what you might call chums, Lee Allan."

"Sure not . . . thank the Lord! But we ain't fighting each other just at the present time, either. It's 'king's ex,' old-timer . . . till further notice."

Bob Farrow lay back and did some rapid thinking. He had never known Lee Allan, save by reputation. He could not fathom the mystery of this mercy; he felt dazed and uneasy, and he watched the outlaw covertly.

When the bacon was done, they ate, not as comrades but in stony silence. Allan did many things for the comfort of Bob, and refilled his coffee cup twice, saying only: "Drink lots . . . yuh got a hard day ahead with that game leg uh yours." At this Bob wondered more.

He watched Allan divide the pack, and tie a part behind the saddle of his horse — and thought it meant desertion in cold blood. He watched him bring a rude, newly made travois such as Indians use to drag burdens, and fasten it to the pack saddle on the pony. He did not quite know what to think of that, but leaned to the belief that Allan was a past master in refined cruelty and meant to keep him alive for a while — for what purpose he could not guess. He made no protest, and fought to keep back the groans when he was transferred to the travois, blankets and all.

The day dragged interminably, although Farrow dozed part of it away. The travois was not as excruciating a mode of travel as he had feared, although his leg hurt cruelly at times. The way seemed strange — he had no doubt they were penetrating farther into the wilderness. They wound through coulée bottoms and narrow gulches for the most part, on account of the travois. He could not help seeing that Allan was very careful, and made the trip as easy as possible.

That night, when they had eaten and the campfire of sagebrush was throwing fantastic lights and shadows upon them, Bob broke his silence with a question.

"Allan, on the dead level . . . what're you doing it for?"

"That's my affair," said Allan shortly, and the conversation closed abruptly.

The next day just after sundown, they stopped in the shelter of a hill that seemed familiar. Bob looked at it long and reflectively. He did not say anything — then. He was weak and feverish, and he thought he must be mistaken.

Then Allan spoke quietly in the undertone he must have learned in those two years of outlawry. "It's pretty hard on yuh . . . but if yuh think you can stand it, we'll make a night move. It's that or lay over till tomorrow night . . . and yuh need care."

Bob caught his under lip sharply between his teeth to steady himself. "I'm dead next to you now, partner," he said a bit shakily. "You're taking me *home.* Don't you know the risk? If anybody gets sight of yuh . . . that ten thousand'll look like a gold mine."

"I'm only going to take yuh as far as the ferry. I'll hold up that old red-whiskered rube and make him take care of yuh." Allan spoke roughly, but the roughness was not very deep, and Bob was not fooled. He stretched out a shaking hand and gripped

77

Allan's fingers.

"You're a better man than I am," he said simply. "You're white. I didn't know yuh, or I wouldn't have come out here. You're . . . *white*."

"No." Allan's tone was bitter. "I'm ten thousand dollars' worth of menace to the peace and dignity of Montana! I'm a blot that the law'd be tickled to death to wipe off the earth. I ain't human. I'm just . . . an outlaw!" It was a cry for justice, and as such Bob read it.

"Look here," Farrow began, after a silence. "You mustn't go any farther. I can manage alone. If you'll fix the bridle on the pony and let me have the reins, I can drive him. Or anyway, he'll go straight home . . . straight to the ferry. He's dead gentle."

"Not on your life. I may be all that my reputation calls for, but I never quit a job till it's done. I started out to land you at the ferry," Allan said in the aloof tone Bob Farrow had come to know so well.

Bob said no more for a time. Then: "I hate to have you ranging out in those god-forgotten hills. It ain't a fit life for a dog. I wish. . . ."

"I'm through here," Allan confided. "I'm sick of plugging posses and raising particular hell by my high lonesome. I've got that ten

78

thousand to help me out. I'm going to drift, partner, soon as I see yuh at the ferry. I wanted to get yuh down here and have some fun with yuh . . . was why I wrote that note. That . . . that starving business was just a bluff . . . I wouldn't do that to a coyote. It was a josh. I knew yuh couldn't get me in a thousand years . . . but I knew I could deal *you* misery, and never touch you."

"You sure succeeded," Bob answered dryly, thinking of those sleepless nights and nightmare days. "I can savvy a trick like that," he went on after a minute. "You had a cinch, and you knew it. But what gets me is why you're doing *this*."

A flame leaped up from the fire and lighted Allan's face; his dark eyes glowed in the glare, then he stood, moved back into the shadow, and looked away to the horses. "We'd better be drifting if we want to get to the ferry before daylight," he said. He walked a few steps from the fire, stopped, then turned and came back. He stood a minute without speaking.

"You . . . said . . . she cared a lot." He went hurriedly back and brought up the horses, and lifted the travois ends gently, so as not to hurt Farrow.

When the boys of the Flying U clanked into
Rusty Brown's place, they found the air
already vibrant with the voice of a man —
not a large man as men go, but a man with
a large voice. The barber and two sheepmen
and the hotel dishwasher were listening very
attentively, and Rusty Brown was leaning
his stomach upon the bar and gazing
straight at the face of the speaker, so ab-
sorbed that he did not even nod at the
Happy Family. Indeed, Rusty's glance spoke
annoyance at the interruption.

The stranger looked at them casually,
observed their chaps and spurs, and waved
his glass toward them inclusively.

"Now, yuh see, it's just as I been telling
yuh," he remarked, at the full capacity of
his lungs. "Here's a bunch that I'd call near-
cowpunchers . . . and, if they're as truthful
as they ought to be, they'll bear me out in
it. I leave it to them if the real range ain't

flattened out like a busted circus balloon. I leave it to them if cowpunchers . . . real ones . . . ain't scarcer right now than breechclout Indians. I'll bet yuh all yuh dare, they don't even pretend they're doing more than make a bluff at it.

"Why, I quit the Coconiño country because it was getting too blame' tame and civilized yuh couldn't so much as shoot the lights out in a dance hall, or any little thing like that, without being run in . . . *run in,* mind yuh . . . and *fined,* by cripes!" He paused while Rusty was refilling his glass.

The Happy Family lined up silently, their faces impassive.

"And as for bad hosses," went on he of the voice, smacking his lips and waving the glass again, "honest to grandma, I've just about give up riding altogether. Time was when yuh could get out and have a run for your money, but the benches they lead out to yuh these days . . . less said the better! I wouldn't insult my saddle by throwing it across their spines. Honest to grandma, I've been a lot tempted to stake myself to a bicycle. They've got more ginger to 'em than nine-tenths uh the hosses nowadays."

Pink at this point simply had to speak or burst. "I suppose you could ride almost any kind of a horse, couldn't you?" he ventured

81

admiringly.

The stranger turned slowly, and looked pityingly down upon Pink. "Little one," he said after a minute, "nothing but your youth and innocence could save yuh after them words. Don't ever repeat 'em. Since yuh ask me in your ignorance, I will say that the hoss don't walk that I can't ride in my sleep. While I'm indulging in personal history, I might add that I'm a mighty bad man to pick a fuss with. My enemies was all good friends uh mine down in Arizona, whilst I was around. I'll pass over your question, as I said, and I'll let yuh drink with Bud Welch, the slickest rider and roper, and the damnedest fighter yuh ever touched glasses with."

Pink clinked glasses with him, and looked impressed. "I suppose you're a fine shot, too," he prompted in his soft, girlish voice.

"Well, now, yuh never seen any real shooting done, little one, if yuh ain't seen *me* twirl the six-gun. If yuh'd hold a dime out between your thumb and forefinger, I'd put a hole in the middle at ten paces without your knowing when it happened . . . at fifteen paces I could do it. At twenty" — he stopped impressively — "I wouldn't guarantee not to trim your nails up once in seven or eight times. Want to try it?"

"I . . . I don't believe I've got a dime that needs punching today, thank you." Pink blushed, and edged away from him.

"I could clip the fire off that cigarette uh yours as far as I could see it," asserted the man who could do things, whirling and glaring at Slim with eyes that were of a pale, unpleasant blue, and that stood out upon his face like the eyes of a frog.

"By golly, I guess you can wait till you're asked!" snorted Slim, growing purple to the ears.

The man glared again, then grinned in a way that startled one, so white and even were his teeth, and so nearly did his mouth approach his ears when he stretched his lips in a straight, long gash clean across his face.

Slim backed involuntarily and said: "Well, by golly!"

"I told yuh these ain't nothing more than tin imitations of the real thing," said Bud Welch triumphantly to Rusty. "Why, down where I come from, they made me plumb weary plugging dimes for pocket pieces. The girls down there used to hold up dimes for me and then string 'em on ribbons for bracelets, and count to see which had the most, and chew the rag over which one stood the farthest off whilst I plugged their dimes. Honest to grandma! I'm getting kinda sorry I drifted north. You're a heap more tamer here than they are down there . . . and I can't say no worse. I expect I'll find myself teaching a young ladies' class in Sunday School come next Sunday."

"We haven't any Sunday School in Dry Lake," remarked Pink deprecatingly.

"Well, by cripes!" retorted Bud Welch, elaborately disappointed. "And that there's a plumb shame . . . seeing the infant class is all assembled."

The Happy Family shifted uneasily, not sure whether it would be beneath their dignity to resent this blatant stranger.

"Say, you're a real wolf, aren't yuh?" said Andy Green, with a smile.

"I sure am, old-timer. Do yuh want me to stick my nose in the air and sing m'war song?" flashed the other. "Only, I ought to tell yuh that I don't howl unless I mean business. Fists or guns, it's all the same to me, by cripes!"

"Don't get excited," purred Andy. "We're some bad ourselves, but we don't eat strangers . . . so long as they're polite and remember their manners."

"Meaning what?" inquired Bud sharply.

"Meaning anything . . . meaning nothing. Say, boys, who was doing all that big talking about billiards a mile or two back? I see the

84

table's empty."

They took the hint, and turned their backs, literally and figuratively, upon Bud Welch. He stared after them, opened his amazing mouth to speak, and turned instead to Rusty. So they got rid of him and his pretensions.

"I'd like to have taken a fall out of that big-mouthed jasper . . . only it would flatter him up too much to take him serious," observed Pink disgustedly.

"He's sure big medicine. I've bumped into that brand of human before," said Andy. "They're plumb wearisome to listen to."

"I betcha he couldn't ride Pink's old Toots, even!" asserted Happy Jack, and thereby precipitated argument of another sort with Pink.

After an hour or so of more or less amicable wrangling around the pool table, they returned to the front part of the saloon, but the boastful one was gone; they did not even miss him and his voice. They were sufficient unto themselves, and they had amusement in plenty without listening to imaginary virtues and accomplishments. Besides, the breed was not uncommon, even in that land where men were numbered by the dozen instead of by the thousand.

Later, when they were back in camp and

were lying around in the grass with their hats tilted against the slanting rays of the sun, Chip Bennett rode leisurely up to the tents, and beside him was another.

"So help me Josephine, it's that big-mouthed gazabo from Arizona!" cried Pink, looking up in disgust.

"I betcha Chip's went and hired him," added Happy Jack misanthropically. And for once, Happy was right.

"Mamma!" sighed Weary, moving his head into the shade. "I'm going to strike Chip for a raise in my wages. If I've got to listen all summer to that frog-eyed terror from Coconiño County, they've got to pay me extra."

"Hello, children!" greeted Bud Welch loudly. "This here looks almost like the real thing . . . from a distance. Honest to grandma, yuh look just like a magic-lantern view . . . 'cowboys on the plains at sunset'. It's a shame yuh can't be took just as yuh are. You'd sure make a hit when some four-eyed sky pilot throwed yuh on the sheet at a church entertainment, with ice cream and lemonade after the show." He smiled his wide smile.

Pink, gritting his teeth, half arose from where he lay, but Andy Green pulled him back. "Don't get excited," he murmured close to Pink's ear. "The higher he soars, the farther he'll have to drop. Let him alone . . . we'll take all that out of him when the sign's right."

The Happy Family may not have recognized telepathy as an exact science, but Andy's viewpoint seemed to have been unanimously adopted, for no one resented the banter openly. Happy Jack did say — "Aw, gwan!" — but the ejaculation was involuntary.

"No, sir, I don't 'gwan'," said the newcomer with a grin. He came over and squatted upon his heels, reached mechanically for Pink's book of cigarette papers, and otherwise deported himself as a man quite at home with them. "I don't 'gwan', because I've give my word to stay with yuh and help yuh out . . . and learn yuh some things. Anybody got a match handy?"

"Couldn't yuh give us absent treatment?" hinted Jack Bates.

"I might . . . if yuh learnt easy enough. Say, how are things up this way, anyhow? This much of an outfit?"

They did not like him and his lordly ways, but his tone had changed with the last two sentences, and he seemed disposed to come down to their humble level and talk like an ordinary human being who did not know quite everything. So they met him on the common ground of range gossip, and treated him much better than they thought he deserved.

It is true that when the talk drifted to riding — a favorite topic with men who spend their days in the saddle — Bud Welch grew once more boastful and laughed at the assertion of Happy Jack that the Flying U owned some "bad actors".

"Honest to grandma, I'd be willing to tackle anything yuh got in your cavvy, bareback, and with nothing but a rope on his nose!" he jeered. "I sized up the bunch when we rode past . . . there's nothing there, boys. I know a bad hoss when I see him."

"Yuh do?" queried Andy Green, thinking of Weaver, the blue roan he had ridden with much stress at the Northern Montana Fair. He had not forgotten the thrill of victory over that unpredictable, creative cayuse.

"Yuh bet I do. The hoss don't live that can fool me. There's a devil looking out uh the eye of every mean hoss . . . if you know enough to read the sign. I don't care how much they play off the ba-ba-sheep in their actions . . . they can't tame down the cunning devil in their eyes. Why I can *feel* it the minute I lay hands on one. It's something yuh can't explain, and yuh can't learn. Yuh've got to be born with the instinct. My old dad was like that . . . he had a big outfit in New Mexico . . . and gambled it away when I was a kid like this young sprig here."

He meant Pink, and Pink's fists doubled unconsciously.

"But he sure could ride . . . my old dad could," Bud continued. "He used to *hunt* trouble, by cripes! If he heard tell of an outlaw *caballo,* didn't make no difference where it was or how much trouble it was to get him, he wouldn't sleep nor eat, scarcely, till he'd got his loop on him. Lord, lord! I've sure seen some riding in my time, boys!"

Deceitfully mild, they let him run on until he grew tired, and not even Happy Jack cut in with the observation that they had a rider or two of their own, and a horse or two that could make any man earn his victory. But before they slept, Pink and Andy Green went unobtrusively to find Chip and take him where they might have a word or two in private.

"Say," began Pink, when they were well out of hearing, "do yuh know anything about that Coconiño terror that's telling it so scary to the bunch?"

"No," said Chip, and glanced through the dusk toward where the voice of Bud Welch sounded, monotonously aggressive. "He

89

struck me for a job, and he claimed to know all about punching cows, so I hired him. What's wrong with him?

"Nothing," put in Andy, "only he's sure been making big medicine ever since he struck camp . . . and down in Rusty's he was running off at the face about the things he could do. He's one of them gazabos that talk big and act small. I know the breed. He's got lots of imagination and a pair uh leather lungs to proclaim himself with, and nothing to back 'em up. He's missed his calling . . . where he'd ought to be is barking for the side show of a three-ring circus."

Chip grinned. "Maybe so. But I don't own a show uh that size and description, so I can't put him where he belongs. He'll have to be just a plain, ordinary stock hand while he stays with this outfit. Did he send you fellows here . . . ?"

"By gosh . . . no!" Andy pinched out the fire on the cigarette he was smoking, and ground the half-burned tube under his heel. "What I want is to lend him The Weaver. He's been mourning because there ain't any bad hosses to ride, no more . . . nothing with ginger to 'em. I kinda felt sorry for him, he feels so bad about it. So I just thought I'd spare The Weaver out uh my string for a while. I kinda thought he might have *ginger* enough. . . ."

"You . . . you devil!" Chip had heard part of what Bud Welch had been declaiming, and he grinned again. "Are you willing to take chances on breaking the fellow's neck?"

"Oh, *I* wouldn't hurt him . . . not! Yuh see, he claims to *like* mean hosses. . . ."

"And Pink here is all nerved up to sacrifice Nigger-White, I reckon!"

"Yuh ring the bell," said Pink, with a dimpling smile.

"The chances are," mused Chip, undecided, "he can't ride to amount to anything. I was going to give him a string of gentle ones."

"Don't you do it, Chip," murmured the voice of Weary behind them. "You let him have Glory for a day or two. He's just been handing out the wildest yarn yuh ever listened to about a cayuse he rode one summer. I never heard Andy, even, lie so bold and free as our friend from the south has been doing."

"Say, Chip!" came the voice of Irish cautiously from the gloom. "When yuh give Big Medicine his string in the morning, just stake him to Piebiter, will yuh? I can spare him, all right, and. . . ."

"Well, I'll be hanged," muttered Chip, greatly amused. "Go on to bed, you bunch

91

uh conspirators. I didn't hire that talkative person for you fellows to kill off first thing. Cal," he began sternly as another dim form showed near them, "don't offer me that kicking cayuse you've been threatening to knock in the head. I've had enough rough horses shoved at me in the last five minutes to build up a riding contest."

"Well, if yuh happen to run short uh . . . ," stammered Cal, a little confused because he had fancied he was the only revengeful one in the lot.

"If we're going to ride with that frog-eyed freak, we've got to take some *plumb obliged to!*" growled Andy. "Here's me with that championship belt stowed away in my war bag, and him proclaiming that nobody but him can ride! If he's going to stay in this camp, he's got to ride The Weaver, and ride him straight up . . . or else he's got to sing lower and more mild."

Chip, although tempted, endeavored to be impartial as became the foreman of the outfit. "Now, look here, boys," he said seriously, "you want to remember that we have some work to do . . . we're not out for fun, or to take the conceit out of men that love to talk big. He's got it coming, maybe, but what I want out of him most is straight riding where it will do the most good. *Sabe?*

This isn't any riding contest, yuh know."

He turned and left them, and Cal was ill-natured enough to remark that Chip was afraid to stay, because he knew blamed well he'd give in. There were, Cal said, certain disadvantages in packing around the dignity of a foreman, and there were times when Chip acted haughty as sin, just because he thought he had to. It made Cal tired — so tired that he marched straight off to the bed tent without another word to anyone.

The others, if one might judge from their general attitude toward the world and one another, were tired, also. They had felt sure of the chance to discipline Bud Welch in the time-honored manner of the range, so sure that they had permitted him to say many things that, if there were to be no future reckoning, were scarcely to be endured.

"So help me Josephine, next time he calls me 'little one', I'm going to land on him like a wolf!" exclaimed Pink, his hat crown just even with Weary's forehead.

"I can't say I blame yuh, Cadwolloper. His manner is sure irritating," sympathized Weary. "I wouldn't be none surprised if Andy is building a scheme to let him down on his face, though. Yuh better hold back and see. Maybe yuh won't have to bother with him at all. Maybe someone else will gentle him down."

At daylight they were eating their breakfast hastily. When the sky reddened, the saddle horses came trotting over the hill and rushed down into the rope corral, docile from long custom. Bud Welch, who had brought his riding gear with him from the south, stood smoking beside his saddle, his rawhide rope coiled over his arm. He appeared to be quite business-like and at peace with himself. He grinned widely at any man who would look at him. Pink he was inclined to treat in a fatherly manner, and Pink made signs enough for an Indian council to Chip. But Chip ignored them all, and pointed out a steady-going little bay to Bud.

They watched Bud covertly when he widened his loop, and they were a bit disappointed when he made only one throw and got his horse neatly over the head, but as the little bay never gave any man trouble, there would have been no excuse for missing.

Unenthusiastically Big Medicine saddled the bay and mounted.

With one accord, and without a word of secret discussion, the Happy Family proceeded to catch their "nifties". There are ways of taking the conceit out of a stranger besides mounting him upon something more than he can manage. Even Happy Jack roped a horse he was wont to pass by, the only one in his string that would do more than crow-hop on a frosty morning. Andy hesitated, his rope poised for a cast at The Weaver. It was not fear that made him turn away and cast the loop over the head of a spiteful, flea-bitten gray that had a trick of bolting at unseasonable times. He wanted to save The Weaver for an emergency. Pink, however, saddled Nigger-White; Irish roped out Piebiter, the worst in his string; and Weary chose Glory — and that when Glory had the roll of eye that promised trouble.

So it was a tumultuous group that went careering away from camp toward the sunrise. On heads and hind feet the Happy Family went, riding with deliberately careless poise, conscious to the last nerve of their audience of one — their audience who loped docilely in the rear, depending upon quirt and spur to keep them in sight.

He did not complain, and he was not set afoot because his horse could go no farther. He jogged into camp at dinner time ten minutes behind the others, and he grinned his wide grin at the Happy Family when he rode past them and dismounted at the corral. His pale, protruding eyes seemed paler and more protruding because his face was red with heat and wind, and something indefinable in his general attitude exasperated the Happy Family greatly.

While they were eating in the shady spots around the mess wagon, he volunteered his first remark, speaking in a paternal tone to Pink.

"Say, little one, yuh strike me as being a kid with talents. Uh course, a man couldn't prophesy correct just exactly what yuh'll amount to when you're growed, but I take the risk uh saying that, if you're trained proper by somebody that's competent, you'll likely be able to ride . . . in ten years or so!"

Pink was nearly twenty-four, although he looked eighteen at most. He was also a bronco-fighter with a reputation — a reputation he had earned honestly — and he had that morning made a ride upon Nigger-White that he considered good.

"Sorry I can't say the same for you," he flung back crossly. "Judging from your style and general appearance, and the wild rides you've been making by word uh mouth, it'd take about a hundred years for yuh to learn anything."

Bud Welch, or Big Medicine as he was fast becoming known among them, turned and grinned at the others. "Ain't he the sassy kid?" he asked them indulgently. "His mother'd oughta take a hairbrush to 'im."

The Happy Family did not laugh. Big Medicine was a stranger among them, and he was not popular. Their sympathies were all with Pink.

"Why don't yuh chastise him yourself?" asked Cal pointedly.

"Oh, well, I was a fresh young sprig myself once," Bud explained carelessly. "He'll get over it, if somebody don't kill him off inadvertent some time, when he gets to handing out them rude observations."

Pink suddenly went fighting mad. He jumped up, threw his plate full at Big Medicine, and swore in an extremely adult, masculine fashion.

Big Medicine wiped a splatter of beans off his neckerchief. "Say, I *will* paddle yuh . . . and paddle yuh *good,* by cripes!" he asserted reprovingly. "Yuh sure have got about as poor manners as any kid I ever seen." He set his half-emptied plate carefully down in the grass. "Yuh watch that a minute, Spike," he told Weary, who was nearest, and arose. "I hate to spank such a pretty-looking young one, but, honest to grandma, he's a fright!"

The Happy Family spilled much good food in getting to where they could watch the proceedings. It was well worthwhile, although they never did agree as to just what happened up to a certain moment. Undoubtedly there were many details that they failed to observe, such as Pink's whirlwind method of fighting. They all saw clearly that he started in his usual manner of punching his opponent hard and often — just when he stopped, no one seemed to remember — but the climax was fixed forever clearly in their minds.

When the revolutions ceased, they saw Pink upon his face with his head thrust between two spokes of the cook-wagon wheel — like a pig in a poke — and Big Medicine kneeling upon Pink's legs. He was spanking Pink thoroughly and methodically with his doubled-up hat, and he was admonishing him in his full-lunged voice: "I sure do hate to do this to yuh, little one, but it's got to be did. Bad boys grow up to be bad men if they ain't learnt better whilst they're young, and someday yuh'll thank me for takin' yuh in hand and learning yuh manners before it's too late. Yuh mustn't throw things at folks. It's rude and unpolite. And yuh mustn't sass growed-up folks. Yuh'll git into all kinds uh trouble if yuh don't quit it.

I want yuh to realize that I'm doing this for your good, and not my own individual pleasure. Now get up, and see what a nice boy yuh can be!"

"He's gone to git his gun," Happy Jack croaked to Bud unnecessarily.

"Well, didn't yuh never see a man go after his gun before? What's strange about that?" asked Big Medicine, and sat down again with his plate in his lap to finish his interrupted dinner.

Happy Jack looked at him uncertainly, encountered his pale, staring eyes, and turned abruptly away. No one said a word.

In a minute Pink was back, and he had his six-shooter and looked less than ever like a nice boy. "Damn your rotten soul!" he cried. "Heel yourself, and do it quick, for I'm going after yuh! I wouldn't take that from anybody that stands on two legs."

Big Medicine looked up at him, grinned tolerantly, and took a very large bite of bread. "Now, don't get peevish," he remonstrated, with his mouth full. "I ain't going to hurt yuh no more."

"Oh, you big-talking, big-mouthed thus-and-so!" Pink stormed, standing over him itching for an excuse to shoot. "You that's such a holy terror down in Coconiño County! You that can plug dimes at fifteen paces, and ride anything that ever wore hair, and are such a hell of a fellow all around . . . get up and show us what yuh can do! *I'll* shoot with yuh . . . if yuh ain't scared to try it. I'll give yuh a fair show. I ain't . . ." Pink, the soft-voiced, the angel-faced, became absolutely unprintable.

Big Medicine ate his dinner, watched Pink meditatively, grinned, and said nothing at all — and that in the face of insults and epithets that would make the ears of a dead man tingle, for Pink had a vocabulary to bring results once he was thoroughly aroused. Big Medicine sat and heard himself called a coward, a quitter, and a gabbling braggart who could do nothing but stretch his mouth to his ears. His personal imperfections were dwelt upon in a way that must have been humiliating even to an insensitive man. But he would not get his gun, and he would not fight again with his fists. He would not make a move that would give Pink a chance at him.

When a man with a gun and heart surging with the lust to kill faces one as Pink faced Big Medicine, there are but two things to do — fight and take a chance, or sit tight and say nothing, which is the only trail to a whole skin. No man who is sane and sober will deliberately shoot down another when that other is sitting, quiet and unarmed, before him.

Big Medicine ceased to smile after the first five minutes, and that was the only visible effect Pink had upon him.

"Look here, now!" said Chip calmly at last, grabbing Pink by one quivering shoulder. "Sounds to me like you've said about all the occasion requires, Pink."

Pink twitched his shoulder loose, stuttered over a last biting epithet, and whirled on his heel. He went to the corral where the horses were being held by the wrangler, and picked up his rope. He lurched a bit when he walked, so greatly did his anger possess him. The others followed silently, Big Medicine trailing behind them all.

Pink stepped over the rope that encircled the horses, made an uncertain throw at the first horse of his string that came near enough, missed, and snared instead a horse no man claimed — an "extra" too vicious to be worth much on the range. Why he was in the bunch at all, no one seemed to know or care, except that he could, at a pinch, be ridden if one were willing to risk a broken bone or two.

Pink yanked the loop tight. "I'll just ride yuh, now I've got yuh," he muttered recklessly with an oath, and led the horse, head up, stiff-legged, and eyes rolling protest, from the corral.

The Happy Family looked at him curiously and Weary started well-meant remonstrance, but Pink only swore at him, and led the horse to where his saddle lay on its side.

Twelve feet away, Chip was yielding to a very human desire to take the conceit out of Bud Welch. Bud had sidled up to him, removed his cigarette from his lips, and grinned deprecatingly.

"Say, could yuh manage to oblige me with a real *hoss* this time?" he had asked mildly.

Chip eyed him sidelong, said — "Huh!" — quite audibly, and pointed out The Weaver. "There's that blue roan you can have . . . only he's liable to take some *riding.*"

"Much obliged," said Bud, and straddled the rope corral eagerly.

The Happy Family sent grateful glances toward Chip — glances that he chose not to see — and hurried their own saddling so that they might see the fun when it began, and keep pace with it if it carried far afield. They almost forgot Pink, although he was having trouble with the beast he had chosen to inflict upon himself.

They all mounted and rode away from camp; they did it so uneventfully that Patsy, gazing from the mess wagon, grunted disgust. Over the hill, however, there was another tale to be told.

Chip, with an eye to harmony and believing that The Weaver was going to behave himself after all, began to turn off his men almost at once. Big Medicine he sent with Weary, because he could trust Weary's tongue and temper. Pink was to ride circle with Happy Jack for leader, because Happy, while he might grow purple and hoarse, would not seriously resent Pink's villainous mood — villainous is the only word that properly describes Pink as he was then.

They started off like the spokes in a rudely shaped wheel, and rode leisurely, for the afternoon promised heat unbearable. 100 yards, perhaps, they went when Weary obeyed an impulse and looked back — then jerked his horse around.

"That brute . . . he'll kill him!" he cried sharply.

Across a little washout, Pink's horse was rearing and plunging wickedly, and Pink, still reckless because of his blind rage, was yanking and spurring spitefully. The horse reared again, twisted in mid-air, and came down with a *thud* that they could hear plainly. In an instant he was up, and they saw Pink jerked sickeningly with one foot caught in the stirrup.

Big Medicine gave an inarticulate sort of bellow, whipped something out from under his trouser belt, and fired. The horse across the washout dropped like a leaden thing, and made no move while the Happy Family raced for the spot to free Pink, who was unhurt save that his ankle was bruised and strained.

Pink felt dazedly for his hat, hopped upon one foot to a rock, and sat down, breathing unevenly.

"So help me Josephine . . . I believe he's going to ride him," he said in something like his normal tones, and they all looked to see where he pointed.

Across the wash The Weaver was gyrating, while in the saddle Big Medicine waved his gun erratically, spurring occasionally, and now and then firing a shot into the air. They watched him anxiously. The Weaver "weaved" his worst. He struck the ground aslant, so that the stirrup of Big Medicine almost grazed the grass. Then up The Weaver went, and came down slanting the other way. North he faced, and in the next jump faced south. Big Medicine shook the reins and fired another shot.

It was some time before he rode over to where they were watching, and, when he did, he put The Weaver across the washout nonchalantly, and galloped up to them grinning his wide grin.

"I was just learning this hoss that noise don't hurt to speak of," he explained loudly, and turned his pale, protruding gaze upon Pink.

Pink blushed, remembering the noise he had himself been making not so long ago — the noise that did not appear to "hurt to speak of".

"He's a right nice little hoss," went on Bud, still grinning, "only, if he stays in my string, he's got to git accustomed to the smell uh gunsmoke, by cripes!"

"By golly," blurted Slim, speaking aloud the question that lay heavy on the minds of the Happy Family. "I'd like to know if this here was an accident . . . this hundred yard shot yuh made, and got that killer in the only spot that'd drop him instant. By golly, *I* call it an *accident*."

"Well, say . . . I ain't none accustomed to accidents . . . not with m'six-gun in m'fingers!" bellowed Big Medicine. "By cripes, where would the kid 'a' been by now if I hadn't stopped that hoss instant? Honest to grandma, even if he is a sassy little devil, I like him a heap. I couldn't ride off and watch him drug to death. By cripes, I just couldn't do it!" He glared at them defiantly.

"I betcha yuh couldn't do it ag'in, just the same!" croaked Happy Jack, his mind yet on the round hole just above the ear of the dead horse.

Big Medicine snorted, grinned amazingly, and rode close to Pink. "Say, kid, I hope yuh don't feel hard toward me yet," he said, leaning solicitously over the saddle horn. "I reelize I done a mean thing to yuh, but joshing is something I can't help . . . I go too far with it sometimes, and I know it." He stopped, and his pale, frog-like eyes became actually wistful.

"I like yuh, kid, and if yuh consider I've done yuh any favor" — he jerked his thumb toward the stiffening heap of horseflesh — "yuh can more than square it by forgetting we ever had trouble."

The Happy Family, somewhat embarrassed by this frank exposure of a man's real self, turned and became very argumentative around the dead horse. They did not see the faint quiver of Pink's lips when he reached up and shook hands with Big Medicine.

# The Land Shark

Con Elliott — big-hearted, big-framed Con, who everybody liked and called friend — laid down a half-smoked cigarette and took up a stubby pencil. He went carefully over a scrawly column of figures, adding aloud to make sure there was no mistake, and then did a very simple sum in subtraction. The result was just the same as it had been five or six times before, and he grunted with dissatisfaction.

"It'll shave my pile down to a whisper, all right," he meditated. "But if it's as I think, my credit'll be good, and I can easy make a living and then some. I can take a bunch uh sheep to winter. I hate the stinking, blatting things, but there's money in 'em, all right. And Fanny and me needn't wait any longer. We could get married right off and settle down in a home of our own. I wonder. . . ."

Con reached for the cigarette, found it had gone cold, and relit it rather awkwardly because of a broken left arm that was only half healed. After a puff or two he picked up the local paper and went over the advertisement of a real estate agent, the only one in Bent Willow.

### FOR SALE

**A snap! 2,000 acres rich prairie land all under fence; improved; good buildings; well watered. Good range. $4,000 cash for quick sale. Worth $10,000.**

"If it's the Jones place," mused Con, "it's sure worth the money. Them four big springs'll irrigate half the land, and it's a peacherine of a place for a man to settle down with a wife . . . with Fanny."

He drew a deep breath at the very thought of it — of Fanny pouring the coffee for him in the mornings in that sunny kitchen he pictured, and baking hot cakes, her cheeks flushed prettily with the heat; of looking down the only coulée, with its yellow rim, to where the sun set redly behind tumbled masses of cloud; of riding with Fanny over the smooth, grassy hills and calling it their own — their *home*. It was long since Con had been able to call any place home.

He read the advertisement again, and his hopes read all these things into the brief notice. He sighed wishfully and reached for his hat.

The agent's name was Abe Sterling, and he was fat and blatant and innocent-eyed, and full of guile. No man had ever bested him in business, and of that he boasted openly, with much laughter.

Men called him a shark to his face, and he seemed rather flattered than otherwise. He held that a man should excel in whatever calling he chose. He was in the real estate business; to be in the real estate business meant that you were out to skin your fellow men, and his ambition was to skin the quickest and with the least pain, don't you know?

He greeted Con with loud cheerfulness and a slap upon Con's well shoulder that made him wince.

"Cut it out, man! I ain't in any shape for your pile-driver brand uh welcome," cried Con, adjusting his sling with careful fingers.

"Well, I forgot. Set down. How are yuh anyway? Ain't seen yuh drunk for a month. I hear you're going to get married. That right?" Abe threw back his head, opened his mouth like a yawning catamount, and ha-

haed so that one could hear him half a block.

Con sat, and took a cigarette pack from his pocket. His broken arm prevented his making his own cigarettes, although he had a notion to learn the one-handed Mexican way. He puffed till a blue haze somewhat veiled his features, and then went directly to the point — which was a way he had.

"How about that ad yuh stuck in today's paper . . . about the ranch for four thousand? Is it a plant?"

"Come to get robbed, did yuh?" Sterling laughed again, then drew his upper lip down over his teeth in a way that to the initiated spelled trickery. "You bet your life that ain't a plant! That's the biggest snap I ever handled, now I'm telling yuh. Two thousand acres."

"Oh, I read the ad," Con cut in dryly. "What I want to know is this . . . is it the old Jones place?"

Sterling looked at him with a gleam of understanding quickly veiled by his drooping eyelids. His voice took on an added heartiness, although it lowered perceptibly. "Yass." Sterling always rolled his words out roundly. "Yass, it's the Jones place. I just got the sale of it yest'day, and for certain reasons . . . yuh know, Con, I can't go into details . . . but for certain reasons it's to be put through quiet. How'd yuh guess what place it was?"

"Well, the size of it tallies, and being well watered, and so on. I worked for Jones a month, once. It's. . . ." He was going to say it was sure a snap, but checked himself when he remembered with whom he was dealing. He finished his remark by saying: "It's over on Squaw Creek."

"Yass, over that way," said Sterling, drawing down his lip again. "I tell yuh, Con, if yuh ain't got the money, yuh can't touch it. It must go for cash. I could 'a' sold it las' night, only for that. That's why it's put down so low . . . only four thousand. But even at that, it ain't everyone that can cough up so much at a minute's notice. Now, there was a man in here about an hour ago. He wants the place the worst way, but he didn't have but three thousand. He tried every way to get me to take that and a mortgage or something for the rest, but I couldn't do it, yuh see. I knew he was good for it all right, but I got my orders to sell for cash, don't yuh see. So he's out rustling for that other thousand. Oh, he wants the place, all right . . . wants it bad."

Con took three puffs while prudence whispered, but hope also whispered of a home. "Maybe I might take a notion to buy it," he said with fine indifference. "What'll yuh take for it, Abe . . . cash down?"

Sterling got up and closed the office door mysteriously, not that it was necessary, but it looked important, and he never overlooked any detail that would make for effect. When he sat down again, he hitched his chair closer and leaned forward.

"Well, now, you know what a snap it is at four thousand, Con." His tone was a bit grieved and wholly reproachful. "I suppose you're thinking about the commission, but it ain't much. Jones is as big a thief as I am. Fifty dollars for my effort is all he'd stand for . . . or he'd put it in somebody else's hands. I got to make a living for the kids, yuh know. I dassn't sell for less. If I did, he'd kick and likely throw off on the whole deal, and you'd both be sore at me, and go 'round saying things about 'that old Abe Sterling . . . the darned old shark!' Yuh know I've got a hard enough name as it is, and the Lord knows. . . ."

"Oh, saw off!" Con interrupted. "You'd rob your dead grandmother of her store teeth . . . anybody knows that. But if yuh rob me, you'll sure repent with your head in the ash pile, old-timer. I'd gamble you stand to clear two hundred out uh the deal, and there's no call to lie about it. If it's four thousand, and no less, I'm good for it. Get down to business."

Con rather doubted the story of the man who was out rustling up a $1,000, but he saw no need to chew the rag all day.

"Well, that's all there is to it," said Sterling soothingly. "The place is for sale at four thousand, and, if you've got the money, you get your deed without no red tape. I had it conveyed to me, so there needn't be any delay hunting up Jones and all that. You say yuh know the place, so I won't try to sling any hot air about it . . . you'd catch me up soon as I wandered from the truth. But I can say this, and prove it . . . the title's straight. I can give yuh an abstract."

Con, not being a property owner, had but a hazy idea of the precise nature of an abstract, but he guessed it was something that put a diamond hitch on the ownership. He asked no questions, trusting to his knowledge of the place in question. He wanted it, and he had the money — part honestly earned by selling a bunch of horses, and the remainder honestly won in a poker game the night before: $4,047 he had, to be exact.

It represented his entire capital, with the exception of two saddle horses, his riding outfit, and camp bed. As he had told himself, it would cut his pile to a whisper, but he did not hesitate. He threw away his cigarette stub and spoke briskly.

"If you can give me a clear title," he said, "and it's the old Jones place, it's a go. I'm figuring on getting sheep to winter. It's fine for that."

"Couldn't be beat!" agreed Sterling, pulling his lip down. "Yuh say yuh got the money with yuh? Then we'll fix it right up. Here's the deed. I had it made out yest'day, with a blank space for the name uh the party uh the second part . . . that's you. This here's the description uh the land . . . 'Sections Fifteen, Twenty, and Twenty-One, and the west half of the southwest quarter uh Section Fourteen, Range Three east, Township Ten.' That makes up the two thousand acres."

"Uhn-huh," assented Con, to whom sections and quarters and ranges were as Greek. Although he could find his way over any part of the country in the dark, he could scarcely tell what township he was in, on a bet. "All right, I'll take your word for it . . . which is something that don't happen to yuh very often, Abe."

Sterling was rapidly — one might say hurriedly — writing **Conrad Elliott** in the

114

blank spaces left in the deed. Abe only grunted.

"That other gazabo'll cuss me blue if he comes back here with his other thousand and finds out I've sold the place," he remarked complacently, while he pressed the blotter upon Con's legal name. "He wanted me to hold it for him, but I wouldn't pin myself down to no promise. I ain't as big a liar as yuh might think." Again the yawning catamount laugh, which he checked suddenly. "Well, say! Before I take your money, Con, I want to tell yuh something. I don't want yuh coming back here saying . . . 'Here, yuh lyin' old devil, why didn't yuh tell me the roof leaks?' That house is going to need some fixing, Con. I know I got a hard name. Any man in Bent Willow'll holler . . . 'Abe Sterling,' . . . if yuh ask who's the biggest liar in town. But I want yuh to be satisfied, Con. I'm going to do the square thing before yuh pay down your money and I sign the deed. That roof'll have to be re-shingled, or it ought to be, 'fore winter, anyway. And the corral is down in one or two places . . . it's liable to take yuh half a day to put it in good shape again. You'll have to do some repairing, all right, and I don't want yuh to say I never told yuh."

"I guess it won't stop the sale." Con

grinned. "If it would, you'd be mighty shy of telling me. If it was any other place but the Jones. . . ."

"Oh, it's the Jones place, all right. Old Jones is dead set on selling out and. . . ."

"Well, he's a damn' fool," asserted Con, reaching into his pocket for his roll.

"Yass, that's what I told him. But he wants the money bad, and, well, I'll just call in a couple uh witnesses and sign this here, and close up the deal. Snap, all right . . . told yuh so on the start."

He put his head out of the window and yelled to the first two men he saw. When they were in the office, he read the deed aloud, rapidly and monotonously, rolling the legal phraseology unctuously, to the bewilderment of his hearers.

Con paid the $4,000, and stuffed a very limp little roll of bills back into his pocket, comforting himself with the thought that, if hadn't much money, he had a home, and the owner of such a place as he had just bought would have no trouble establishing his credit.

With long steps and a light heart he headed straight for the kitchen of the St. Paul House, a rather plebian establishment where Fanny Mallory was hashing for $25 a month — and where, Con told himself, she would hash no more. She would keep house for him, and bake his hot cakes in the seclusion of their own sunny kitchen.

He had hated, from the time he first fell in love with her Irish eyes, the thought of her waiting upon all sorts of men, and dreamed of the time when her attentions would begin and end with himself.

As he entered the steaming kitchen where a saffron-colored Chinaman was pattering about, making preparations for dinner, Fanny kicked the dining room door open and came out with a great tray load of dirty dishes. Con felt much inward resentment at the sight. It wasn't fit work for his Fanny.

"Hello, Con!" she greeted briskly, setting down the tray. "That's the last of breakfast, thank goodness! Where've you been all morning?"

Con answered by saying he would like to see her for a few minutes. Fanny, perhaps divining something unusual, promptly led the way back into the deserted dining room and the corner that, experience told her, was quite beyond range of the peephole in the door.

Naturally Con indulged in those little preliminaries that are the inalienable rights and privileges of engaged young men before he told her how he had bought a place that

117

would make a dandy little home, and that her days of hashing — thank God! — were over — and would she marry him that evening?

After much coaxing, and a further indulgence of the inalienable rights and privileges, Fanny would. In truth, she would do anything Con really wanted her to do, which is a proper spirit for engaged young women — and she was horribly sick of hashing; she said so.

In half an hour it was all settled. They would be married that evening, and in the morning Con would hire a rig and they would drive out to look over their new ranch and make arrangements for immediate possession. Sterling had assured Con that he could move onto the place as soon as he liked, and they decided that Con must hire a man to do the work until his arm was strong.

Con loved to carry out his ideas while they were yet warm with enthusiasm, and his mood was almost hilarious before he left the dining room.

For the rest of that day, Fanny's hashing was far from satisfactory. She moved mechanically about her work, and didn't know half the time whether she was serving tea or coffee, or both.

Surely such absent-mindedness was inevitable, for, when she was not debating whether she should be married in her last year's 4th of July dress, which was white, or in her new, pale blue silk waist, which had cost $4.98 and had only been worn once to a dance, she was trying to picture just what life would be like on a ranch — their own ranch! — with Con.

For the benefit of chance women readers who are interested in such trifles, I will say that she finally decided — very sensibly in a mere man's opinion — to wear the white dress. Con thought she looked sweet as a peach, and told her so — which was also sensible.

It was twenty-one miles to the Jones place, but they didn't mind that. And once away from the inquisitive gaze of Bent Willow, Fanny did the driving, while Con employed his well arm to better purpose. They talked, and planned, and spooned, and Fanny let the horses poke, and — no, they certainly did not mind the distance.

When they came in sight of the place, Fanny declared that she wouldn't trade places with Queen Victoria — Fanny had forgotten that the good Queen was in heaven. At any rate, she meant to express her unqualified approval of their home. She said it was the prettiest ranch in the country, and Con was a dear, so they drove up to the house in rather an exalted mood.

When they stopped at the door, Jones himself appeared, to give them a Western welcome, which means that he insisted upon their stopping to dinner, at the very least.

"You bet we will," Con accepted heartily. "We just drove out to take a look at the place . . . this is my wife. We was married last night." Con added visibly to his height while he said it. "We've bought the place, Jones. I knew it was a snap, yuh see, and just what we wanted for a home. We'll talk about moving in, after a while."

It was a long speech for Con, but he was in a particularly exuberant mood, and the silence of Jones kept him talking.

To be exact, the eyes of Jones bulged with puzzled astonishment, but he had much presence of mind, and told Mrs. Elliott to go right in and make herself at home while they put up the team.

When she had gone, he faced Con determinedly.

"I never knowed yuh to be much of a josher, Con," he said, "so I'd like to know what 'n' all yuh mean by buying my place! I ain't sold no place. When I want to sell out, I'll let yuh know it. This little old ranch is good enough for me."

"Why, I sure bought it," argued Con, with lengthening jaw. "I got it off Sterling yesterday . . . and paid four thousand in hard coin for it. He said he was your agent."

"Four . . . thousand . . . dollars? For this ranch? I wouldn't take ten thousand for it!"

"Well, I said you was a darn' fool." Con pushed back his hat, bewildered. "Abe Sterling is an old shark, everybody knows that," he added dazedly, "but he sure wouldn't dare sell another man's ranch . . . that's too darn' rank. I . . . say, Jones, come on to the stable. I . . . I don't want my wife to hear . . . right after being married."

He led the way with long strides, while Jones followed thoughtfully, leading the horses.

At the stable, where no feminine eyes or ears could possibly be shocked, their dialogue became quite free of restraint — which did not hasten a thorough understanding. Con insisted that he had bought the Jones ranch, and Jones reiterated that he had not sold it, and he'd be several impolite things if he ever did sell it. For five minutes it looked and sounded very much like a quarrel.

Then Con's retentive memory came to the rescue. "Man," he urged, "I got a deed for it, all right . . . with a couple uh fellows for witnesses. It was 'Sections Fifteen, Twenty, and Twenty-One, and the west half of the southwest quarter of Section Fourteen, Range Three east, Township Ten.' Is that the brand uh this ranch, or ain't it?"

"It ain't," said Jones decisively. "Not by a long shot. I'm in Range Four, Sections . . . say, by thunder! Yuh bought that old Jimpson place over the ridge there, six or eight miles! Yuh mind the place, where they was going to have a flowin' well that'll make the desert to bloom, and got straight alkali juice that ruined what little land was fit to raise stuff on. It's been flowing regular for six or eight year now, and what ain't plumb gone to granny with that alkali is high gravel ridges that'd starve a mountain sheep to death. A tenderfoot named Jones got soaked on that . . . bought it on the strength of a lot uh hot air, same as yuh done. Well!"

Con did not say "well". He said other things — and the saying lasted a good fifteen minutes. After that he felt something like calm.

"Yuh mind what I say, Jones," was his first publishable remark. "I'll get even with that old land shark, if it takes me a thousand years!"

Fanny took the news hard. She declared over and over that she "would like to scratch Abe Sterling's eyes out." I hope no one will consider Fanny savage and unladylike — she was Irish, and she was deeply wronged.

They drove dispiritedly over to their ranch, which no longer filled them with the gloat of possession. Undoubtedly it was theirs, every stony, barren foot of it, but they did not tell each other so with proud repetition. Instead, they glared vengefully at the high ridges with the outcroppings of yellow sandstone, and invented new and horrible things they would like to do to Abe Sterling.

What seemed to Con the most intolerable insult of all was the discovery that Sterling had, in one particular, spoken truth. The roof certainly needed fixing! It not only leaked, it threatened to collapse utterly. The corrals were lying, for the most part, flat upon the ground, and the sheds sagged drunkenly.

"The nerve of him!" gritted Con. "To tell me they needed repairs! Repairs!" He looked away down the hill coated with a white crust of alkali, and cursed Abe Sterling in his heart.

Fanny sat down upon the rickety doorstep — their own doorstep! — and cried. Never had she dreamed, she who had never owned anything but her tawdry clothing, that the ownership of a 2,000-acre ranch could be such mockery.

"You never mind, little woman," Con comforted, stirred out of his own gloomy mediations by her sobbing. "It's highway robbery, and worse, for the law can't buy in and put him where he belongs . . . in the pen. He'd better 'a' rolled me. I could have more respect for him if he had. It was a plant, from start to finish. And I can play that game as well as he can, although maybe I ain't had the practice. If I wanted to rob a man, I'd get out with a gun and stick him up honest."

"The . . . bald-headed . . . old . . . thief!" interjected Fanny, gulping.

"Sure he is, but you wait. I'll get my money back with the biggest interest ever paid. Don't cry, girlie, you watch my smoke."

Secretly, however, Con did not feel so sure of getting even.

They drove moodily back to the town they had left so blithely, and because Con was crippled and without funds, Fanny went back to hashing in the St. Paul house. The boarders accused her of being cranky and snappish, but who could blame her? Certainly not Con.

Con himself, grown crafty through the school of bitter experience, went out the next morning in search of Sterling. Not that he was in any condition to do anything like justice to the occasion of their meeting, but because he knew that Sterling would be expecting a display of some sort.

Con Elliott was not known among his fellows as a "bad man", and upon that fact Abe Sterling had counted much. For all that, he was careful not to be in his office when Con arrived and left tokens of the visit; that is, he kicked the table over, and emptied the ink bottle over what papers looked important, and threw the office chair out of the window without regard for glass or sash. Then he went in search of the fugitive.

He found Sterling in the office of the St. Paul House, and walked up to him, ominously calm. "Old-timer," he said, "I've got a settlement to make with you, and I ain't in the shape for it just at present, but put it down that your pay day's sure a-coming."

"Well, now, Con, yuh needn't blame me." Sterling edged toward the door. "I never asked yuh to buy that place. Yuh come to me and wanted it, and I sold it to yuh. That's my business."

"Yes, your business is the double-cross, every time yuh can catch an honest man with his back turned. Why, yuh. . . ."

"Now look here, Con." Sterling spoke pacifically. "I read yuh the description b'fore I took your money, didn't I? Yuh know I did. And yuh said yuh knew the place. How was I to guess yuh was laboring under a mistake?" His eyes were wide with in-nocence — the exaggerated innocence that betrays conscious but impenitent guilt. "I never told yuh a thing that wasn't so, did I, now? It's well watered . . . yuh know that . . . and I told yuh the roof leaked. . . ."

"That'll do, Abe. Yuh needn't rub it in." Con was still dangerously calm. You could scarcely have told that he was angry, except for his clenched fist. "I won't kill yuh, because I've got a wife to think about, and yuh ain't worth the trouble. When my arm is ready for business, it'll be a pleasure to work your face over till you'll have to be identified to your own looking-glass. But in the meantime, I done a few things to your den up the street, and I'll just kick yuh up there to see the wreck."

He did so, with the thoroughness that was

characteristic of him. Every man in Bent Willow rushed out to see Abe Sterling flee before his victim while Con's right boot landed regularly, every alternate stride, upon the lower part of Sterling's coat.

When the office door slammed between them, Con turned and went composedly back to the hotel where Fanny had watched him from the dining room window.

"I ain't through with him yet," he told her grimly. "The hostilities have got to rest here for the present, and I guess that'll hold him for a while. Anyway, it's eased my mind some considerable."

It was on a July morning when Abe Sterling found a stranger waiting upon his office steps. Business was none too brisk, so the stranger was greeted with Sterling's warmest smile. The man went in with the straight back of a consciously important person, and seated himself patronizingly in the office chair.

Sterling sat down on a corner of the table, and swung one leg to show how little he was awed by the magnificence of the other. He offered him a cigar, but the stranger waved it aside with a supercilious, bediamonded little finger, and got out a silver-mounted cigar case that had a monogram on the outside, and on the inside a half dozen cigars, which Sterling instinctively appraised as better than he himself could afford.

"Try one," invited the stranger affably. "Import 'em myself . . . never smoke anything else."

After a tentative puff or two, Sterling understood why.

"Well," began the stranger after a minute, "we'll come down to business. I'm in a hurry . . . lots to see to yet . . . want to leave on the three o'clock train. Stranger here, don't know a soul. You've got your sign out as a dealer in real estate, so I came to you after a little information. Want to know who owns a certain tract of land, out east of here." He waved the bediamonded finger vaguely. "Been out there looking around . . . ahem!" His brows pinched warily together. "I looked up a section corner or two . . . Twenty and Twenty-One, but I can't tell you the range . . . went alone, for certain private reasons."

Sterling's upper lip drew down over his teeth. He suspected something behind this vague preliminary, and, by the droop of his lids, he was ready for any sort of development. "What sort of place was it?" he asked mildly. "Wild range, or under fence, or what?"

"Under fence, yeah. Mighty lot of it, by the look. Few old buildings at the top of a . . . er . . . coulée, you call them, and a well that's slopping alkali water by the barrel all over the place. Bad thing that . . . alkali. I'll give five dollars if you'll tell me who owns that place, and where I can find him . . . at once."

The lip went down again like an eyelid. It was as if Sterling's mouth had a habit of winking. "Well, now, pardner, yuh needn't throw good money away. I'll tell yuh for nothing. I own that place myself."

Of course — oh, well, a lie, more or less, couldn't matter to a man like Sterling!

"Oh!" The stranger covered his surprise admirably and flicked the ashes from his cigar quite nonchalantly. "Well, it's a poor layout, but I've taken a notion. Do you want to sell it?"

"Well, now, I don't know!" Sterling blew a mouthful of aromatic smoke toward the grimy ceiling. "I believe that land'll be worth something to me some uh these days. I've found indications of . . . er. . . ." He stopped and looked very crafty, and wished he knew just what the stranger had up his sleeve.

*"Hmm."* The other nodded. "Maybe you have. But indications of . . . er . . . anything . . . can't always be written with the dollar mark in front. What'll you take for that tract . . . cash down?"

"What do you want it for?" Sterling was holding off and praying for light.

The stranger turned his hand and idly watched the sparkle of his diamond. "Going to raise sweet potatoes," he drawled insolently.

Sterling took up the gauntlet. "Well, now, sweet potato land is worth money . . . in this state," he retorted slyly. "But everybody'll tell yuh, I'm a shiftless cuss, and the Lord didn't make me for a farmer. So I'll give yuh a bargain. You can have that hull tract . . . two thousand acres . . . for eight thousand dollars." He said it innocently, too!

"Too much." The stranger shook his head and pursed his lips, and continued to admire his ring. "Better come down a notch, you can't work me, you know."

"On the dead, I won't make ten percent profit on the place at that figure. When you count up the taxes and all . . . and I've hung onto that piece uh land like grim death, just on the strength of them . . . indications, uh . . . er . . . sweet potatoes. Why, just yesterday a feller come to me and offered. . . ."

"Eh? Yesterday?" The stranger sat up and took his eyes from the ring. Then he pulled himself together and resumed his position. "Come now, what's your lowest figure? I'm in . . . er . . . something of a hurry and. . . ."

"Eight thousand." Sterling clung doggedly to his price.

"Make it seven thousand, and it's a go."

"Couldn't. Couldn't possibly do it. The other feller offered. . . ."

"Split it, then. Seventy-five hundred is all I've got orders . . . er . . . is all it's worth."

Sterling yielded reluctantly. "Oh, all right, I won't haggle with nobody. Seventy-five hundred goes. Hang it! A man can't make a living in the land business no more."

"Well, my time's valuable. You can give me a deed now . . . at once? I must get after that other business."

The stranger had already drawn out a roll of bank notes and was chewing his cigar stub excitedly.

"Well, now, I keep all my important papers in the bank, and the deed to that tract is among 'em. I'll have to get it, to make sure uh the description . . . and the bank ain't open." Sterling consulted his watch and frowned. "Say!" he said. "You go on and tend to that other business, can't yuh? And come back after the deed, say . . . well, say 'leven or half past? I'll have it ready by then, and . . . it's the best I can do."

The stranger eyed him suspiciously. "Going to hunt up that other man and try to get a rise? No, you don't! Here. I'll just pay you a hundred to bind the bargain, and you give me a receipt. See? Business is business. And you have that deed ready by noon, or you forfeit a hundred dollars. Write it into the receipt, or you don't go."

Sterling didn't much like that; he considered that he was taking quite enough risk as it was. But the stranger looked as if he were in the habit of getting things as he wanted them, so the clause went into the receipt, and Sterling signed it.

He watched until the stranger had turned a corner, and then hurried not to the bank, but to the St. Paul House, where Con Elliott was tending bar that he might be under the same roof with Fanny while they worked to retrieve their evil fortune.

"Say, hello, Con! Come outside a minute." Sterling was not in the mood nor had he the time to be diplomatic.

"Sure! Come to get that thrashing I promised yuh? I was just telling the boys I guess my arm is well enough to. . . ."

"No, Con, look here. I know I done a mean trick by yuh, but yuh was so dead easy, I just couldn't resist. I know you're laying to get even. . . ."

"You can sure gamble on that, old-timer!"

"Well, I've concluded to do the square thing, and head yuh off. I know I ain't no match for yuh in a fight. I stand ready to give yuh back your four thousand and take the place. Next time I'll work it off on some stranger. It wasn't hardly square to do an old friend that way . . . I know it."

"Why, yuh little dear!" gurgled Con, the acme of derision. "You've got a wooly white coat over your coyote skin, and want me to admire yuh, and say how sweet and pretty yuh look! If you stand ready to cough up my four thousand, it's a cinch some other misguided mortal is going to lose more than what I did. What do you take me for . . . a darn' fool? You can have that place, old-timer, for six thousand cold dollars, or you can take a most outrageous thumping for coming down here and insulting my intelligence."

"No, Con, yuh must be crazy." Sterling's jaws went flabby and gray. "Six thousand, man! Why. . . ."

"So I guessed right. That physiog uh yours says so. Yuh must 'a' put the price 'way up, but I'll stand by what I said. You can have it for six thousand, and you're welcome to all yuh get over and above that. That's my last word . . . my ultymatum. Yuh know me."

Sterling did, but in spite of his knowledge, which should have taught him the futility of it, he spent all the time he dared and all the arts and arguments he knew, trying to persuade Con to mercy.

At 11:00 Abe Sterling gave it up, went to the bank, and drew $6,000 — the operation was to him much like drawing six molars without an anesthetic — and laid the money reluctantly in Con's left hand, receiving at the same instant a deed, duly signed and witnessed, from Con's right hand. And Con had called a crowd around him to see the fun.

Sterling almost ran back to his office, sick with fear that he would be too late. He felt that the stranger in such an event would be as adamant as was Con. However, the man had not returned. He drew up another deed, leaving a blank space for the stranger's name, which he had forgotten, looked at his watch, and found it yet lacked ten minutes to twelve. He drew a long sigh of relief, wiped the perspiration from his face, lit a cigar, and sat down to wait.

So far as I know, he is still waiting.

At ten minutes to twelve, Con Elliott counted out ten twenties and laid them down on the bar before the stranger. "Good boy, Tony! Yuh sure ought to quit gambling and go on the stage. Pretty smooth . . . that hundred-dollar forfeit play! Too bad yuh can't stay and watch old Abe gore the sod when he finds out the plant. Bent Willow will sure throw it into him aplenty over this deal. What'll yuh have, boys? It's on me."

"I'll take whiskey for mine," said Tony, waving his little bediamonded finger jocularly. "And say! Any of you boys got a real estate deal yuh want put through for yuh? It sure beats faro for getting the coin. I'm some tempted to make it my long suit. Here's how, Con!"

# LAW ON THE FLYING U

"You, Rummy! Get away from that fence before I brain yuh with a rock!"

Chip yelled too late. Or perhaps his voice served to crystallize a vague desire into action. Whichever it was, the words seemed to lift the big chestnut colt over the pasture fence in the clean, effortless flight of an antelope clearing a buckbrush blocking its way. Heels flickered in the sun as the colt kicked and squealed a try-and-catch-me challenge — and Rummy was off down the coulée in a flashing gallop, disappearing among the willows of the creek bottom.

"Well, did you ever!" his mother, Silvia, seemed to say, as she threw up her head and stared after the yearling in horrified amazement. She galloped to the fence where he had gone over and sent a peremptory — *Whn-hn-hn-hn-hn!* — after the culprit, no doubt telling him in horse language that he'd better come back if he knew what was

136

good for him.

But Rummy would not deign so much as a whicker of defiance in reply. For three months and more he had stuck right there in the Flying U pasture while the other horses fared forth on a roundup, seeing the world. He had grown almost a third of his size that summer. Another year and he'd be as tall as his mother. He could take care of himself just as well as any horse that ever ran the range. Come back? Nothing doing!

Chip Bennett thought otherwise. And so did Silvia, the mare. It was all Chip could do to keep her back while he led his own private horse, Mike, through the gate with only a lead rope looped over Mike's nose. Chip flung himself on the horse's back and galloped off to the corral, leaving the mare racing up and down inside the fence. She whinnied frantically, little Silver, her newest colt, galloping leggily alongside and adding his shrill call to the uproar she made.

Most of the boys were sprawled on their bunks, or down by the creek in the shade of an old cottonwood, trying to get caught up on sleep. No telling when they'd have another idle Sunday at the ranch until the beef roundup was over, and they were making the most of this lazy afternoon. Chip had gone to the pasture to see his horses, as was his habit, and so he had witnessed the yearling's break for freedom.

He saddled in a hurry, and mounted, taking down his rope as he rode. His language as he did so would be a mistake to repeat. He knew too well the devilment of which that chestnut colt was capable.

Furthermore, Chip had gone to the pasture with the expectation of lounging there in the shade with his back against a tree, resting and watching his pets, and maybe drawing a picture or two — or just taking a nap, if he felt too lazy for anything else. Certainly it had been no part of his plan to chase that damnable Rummy all over seventeen counties in the full heat of the afternoon, for, although they were well into September and had already made a shipment of beef, the days were still hot. The heat of the day, however, was not to be compared with Chip's wrath, which blistered Rummy every step of the way.

This is no story of that chase. Its significance lies at the end of it, more than an hour after its beginning. Rummy had been smart enough to head for rough country, where there was plenty of dodging. He had several minutes' start, and he was fleet as a deer. He was well into the breaks before Chip got a glimpse of him, and he was enjoying himself hugely and meant to keep going.

Then fate played a mean trick on Rummy. Chip heard his shrill whinny down a narrow, winding gulch, followed by the trampling of hoofs — too many hoofs to be just the colt's. The next minute, a rider appeared around a shoulder of the cliff, leading the colt ignominiously behind him.

The meeting was sudden. Chip set Mike back on his haunches and stared, his breath caught in his throat for a moment.

"Why . . . hello, Mase," he stuttered doubtfully, his face hot with embarrassment. "Y-you got Rummy, I see."

"That what you call him? Hello yourself, Chip! Only . . . better call me Mason, will you? . . . Jim Mason, these days."

"Why . . . sure." Chip hesitated, then rode up and put out his hand. "Names don't matter. I'm glad to see you, anyway."

They shook hands gravely.

"I sure didn't expect to see you up here," Mason observed, glancing back at the colt. "I thought it was your brother Wane coming, when I met the gelding back down the gulch. Knew the brand, of course. And I'd heard Wane Bennett was up in this country somewhere. That was over a year ago." He glanced behind him with the unconscious watchfulness of the hunted. "That colt's a dead ringer for the mare your brother used to own."

"Yes." Chip bit his lip, dropped his gaze to Mike's mane. He paused, then launched into an explanation. "You see, I came up looking for Wane after our mother died. I brought up the mare and her colts. Wane . . . he was killed last fall."

Mason swore a surprised and dismayed oath. "I sure liked Wane Bennett. I . . . that's damned bad news, Chip!"

"Plain hell for me," Chip said shortly. "I'm working for the Flying U. You know Jim Whitmore, don't you? From Colorado."

"Heard of him. Never happened to meet him, though. Say, I wonder what's the chance for a job? Think I could get on?"

"Why . . . I think so. Just sent a man to the hospital a few days ago. Had a stampede and a cloudburst, both together, and one man got hurt. We're hiring at the ranch to get organized again. Flood came right down through camp and sure played hell. We've just about got to start at the bottom and get a new outfit together. I guess they could use you, all right. If you want to come on to camp with me, you can damn' quick find out."

Jim Mason shook his head. "I was just kiddin'. I wouldn't want to get you in bad. Your brother Wane was a pretty good friend of mine."

"That's why," Chip broke in. "Wane said he didn't blame you a damn' bit for what happened. And, anyway, I guess it would be safe to tell J.G. the whole story. I know it would, in fact."

"Not on your life! I tell my affairs to nobody, kid, then I don't have to worry about whether there's a leak somewhere."

He got out smoking material and rolled a skimpy cigarette, holding up the limp tobacco sack afterward.

"That's the last of it." He grinned bleakly. "Spent my last dollar for horse feed, back down the trail." He gave Chip a studying look. "Tell you what. I'm Jim Mason, and you don't know me from Adam's off ox. Is that a go with you?"

"Sure, it's a go with me. I'll never forget that you were a friend of Wane's."

"All right. That's for your own protection . . . just in case anything happens. I ain't lookin' for any slip-up, mind. Haven't been bothered for two year and more. Well, lead out, then. You used to be able to keep your trap shut. I'm just a feller that boned you for a job."

"That's all," Chip laconically agreed, and

got down, and put his own rope on Rummy before he started back to the ranch.

He rode in the lead, Jim Mason trailing behind Rummy. Chip didn't want to talk, he wanted to think, but whatever his thoughts were on that homeward ride, they did nothing to change his mind about helping Mase Caplan — a name he must now forget — who had become a mere stranger who called himself another name.

The Flying U boys were lounging in the shade of the bunkhouse, waiting for supper, when the two rode up. Shorty came out of Jim Whitmore's cabin and stood eying the stranger, saying nothing until Chip rode over and stopped before him.

"Here's a man says he wants work," Chip stated in his terse, matter-of-fact way. "Met him headed this way when I was chasing the colt."

And with that he started for the pasture as if he had no further concern in the affair.

"Have to ask the boss, I guess," Shorty was saying.

He stepped to the doorway behind him and leaned his big body inside. What he said was indistinguishable outside, but J. G. Whitmore appeared in a moment, limped to the horseman, and studied him as he went. He gave a noncommittal nod.

"Can you ride?" he asked abruptly. "Had our saddle bunch stole off us this summer, so every string's the rough string. Think you can hold up your end?"

Mason gave his slim body a twist, and spat toward a high weed off to his right. "I'm willing to try it a whirl," he said quietly.

"Uhn-huh."

J.G.'s eyes rested upon the stranger's horse, a shiny black with white stockings all around and a white star on his forehead. "Pretty good horse you're ridin'," he remarked casually. "He yours?"

"He sure is," Mason answered quickly, and laid a hand upon the arched neck where the light gave a sheen like a blackbird's wing. He smoothed the neck with a touch that was worshipful. "They don't come any better than this little horse," he said with a flash of white teeth.

"Looks like he's got good staying qualities," the Old Man rambled on, coming up to stroke the beautiful animal on the nose. "A drifter, ain't he?"

"I'll say he is! I once rode him eighty-five miles between dark and dawn. . . ."

He bit his lips as if he had committed an indiscretion. His dark glance went quickly to J.G.'s face.

"Don't doubt that for a minute. What's

his name?" asked J.G.

"I call him Blackbird . . . Bird, for short."

The horse was nuzzling J.G. in friendly fashion, and receiving a lot of smoothing and petting and straightening of his forelock in return. Mason watched from the saddle.

"Well, git off and turn him in the corral," the Old Man said at last. "We can put you on, I guess, if you're willing to tackle a rough string, but I may as well tell yuh right now, they won't none of 'em be smooth ridin'!"

"I don't know as I ever saw the rough string that was," Mason observed as he swung down.

Most men would have ridden the few rods to the corral. It looked a little as though he wanted to show off his horse, for he walked a dozen steps, and then said softly — "Come on, Bird." — in a tone such as he might have used to a woman.

The horse nodded his head sagely and turned, following his master daintily, with the springy pasterns that bespeak speed and smoothness in a horse. Mason stopped and waited, and Bird walked along the rest of the way with his nose over his owner's shoulder.

J.G. looked after the two meditatively. "You can most generally judge a man by what his horse thinks of him," he said to no one in particular, and went back into the cabin.

In the next few days Mason found his place in the Flying U outfit and kept it. He was a quiet man, and did his work as well as any boss could desire. That he was a lover of horses, the most unobserving speedily discovered, and that his horse, Blackbird, meant more to him than anything else on earth, the Happy Family guessed from the very start.

Chip Bennett loved his horses with an unswerving devotion that set him apart as an unusual sort of fellow, but his affection was lukewarm alongside Jim Mason's worshipful regard for the black horse, Bird. Except when the man was at work and riding a Flying U mount, the two were inseparable.

For instance, Bird was not kept in the pasture with the other horses while the outfit remained at the ranch; he ran loose, feeding quietly as near to his master as he could handily get. He had the run of the camp like a dog, and he made friends with every man who held out a hand to him. So he became a pet, and even Patsy, the cook, surrendered to the animal's ingratiating ways and fed him biscuits whenever Bird thrust his shiny black head and neck in through the doorway and coaxed with his eyes and a reaching lip.

At night, Mason took his thin blanket roll out wherever the grass was good and slept on the ground, while Bird grazed around him. The two would come in together at dawn, the horse walking springily along with his nose thrust over Mason's shoulder — a pretty sight that somehow touched the boys and held them from playing their crude jokes on Mason. He was a queer kind of cuss, they all agreed, and let it go at that.

When the repaired wagons and their loads rattled up out of Flying U coulée to continue the beef roundup, Mason proved beyond all doubt that he could deliver the goods when it came to riding half-broken broncos. And before many days had passed, it was noticed that his rough string was gentling down to the work. The boys watched him covertly, trying to discover what magic he used. Mornings, when the Flying U camp became the scene of an impromptu bucking contest, Mason loped off about his business with not so much as a crow-hop to mar the evenness of his horse's stride.

Among themselves, the Happy Family

discussed the marvel.

"I'd give a dollar to know how he does it," Cal Emmett declared fretfully. "I shore would like to try it on that flea-bitten gray I got."

" 'Why Mary loves the lamb, you know,' " Chip quoted, and walked away from the group before he was tempted to point out a few facts to Cal, whose method with bucking horses was to bear-fight them until they gave in.

"Yeah, but that cussed gray sure ain't nobody's lamb!" Cal called after him in his bellowing voice. "Shorty went and staked Mason to a bunch of sheep to ride. I guess that's the secret of the whole thing. If he had a few of them man-killers I got handed out to me to ride, he wouldn't be goin' aroun' talkin' baby talk to 'em, I tell yuh. Those, he'd talk to 'em with a club . . . what I mean."

Chip swung half around and gave him a single look, and walked on. Not a word did he say in reply to that. He did not need to. Cal was suddenly purple with anger, although he did not say anything, either. He knew well enough what Chip and some others thought of his way of taming broncos.

Perhaps that little wordless encounter

rankled next morning. Anyway, that would account for the mood Cal was in, and for his roping out the gray. The roundup had moved up to one of the Flying U line camps, where a set of stout corrals had been built the fall before for such work. In a small corral, Cal was sweating and swearing, and the gray was sitting back on his haunches with his neck stretched at the end of Cal's rope, rolling his eyes and stubbornly refusing to be led toward the gate.

The rest of the boys were catching their mounts and saddling them with only a normal amount of trampling and swearing, and at the moment no one paid any attention to Cal. But then the gray gave an unexpected lunge forward and nearly knocked Cal down.

"Momma! There'll sure be something doing now!" Weary prophesied to Chip as he came out, and ducked his head again to peer in between the rails.

"Well, if he gets his head knocked off, it'll serve him right," Chip commented.

For perhaps five minutes, however, there was no great excitement within the corral. Cal got the gray outside at last, and, with a glance around to make certain that neither J.G. nor the foreman happened to be at the corral, he led the horse a few panels to one side and tied him securely to a post. Then he went searching for a club.

Chip had already saddled, and was gathering up the reins, ready to mount. As Cal balanced the stout stick in his hand and walked purposefully up to the shrinking gray, Chip set down the foot he had lifted to the stirrup. He looked questioningly across his horse at Weary, who was saddling, nearby. Weary canted a disgusted glance at Cal, looked at Chip, and shook his head. A man had a right to "work a horse over" if he thought the animal deserved it and would learn better manners from the punishment. Unless he went to cruel and inhuman extremes, he must be left alone.

Chip knew that unwritten law well enough, so he bit his lip and led his snorting bronco away from that vicinity, where he could not witness the beating.

"Some of these days I'm going to land on Cal with all four feet," he gritted as he passed Weary. "Maybe that horse needs a dressing down, but. . . ."

"But Cal needn't look like he enjoyed whaling the tar out of him," Weary finished softly. "That's what grinds."

Just then Jim Mason came on the run, his face a mask of fury through which his flaming eyes looked out. He did not say a word.

He grabbed the uplifted club from Cal's hand and knocked him sprawling in the sand.

On all fours, Cal scrambled away from the hoofs of the plunging gray. He got up fairly frothing at the mouth, he was so mad. He went at Jim Mason like a wild man, bellowing threats, and men came running from all directions. Cal was one of those men who fight for the sheer love of combat.

He caught Jim Mason in a terrific rush, bore him back, and threw him heavily. After that it was pretty much of a mix-up for a while, but, in the end, Cal was the one who yelled he'd had enough. Weary and Chip rushed in and pulled Mason off him. Mason was shaking, white as his wind-tanned skin would bleach with emotion, and his eyes still had a glassy look. He staggered to the corral fence and leaned against it while he recovered his wind and stanched the blood streaming from his nose.

"All right," he said in a hoarse, unnatural tone to Chip and Weary. "I kinda lost control of myself, I guess." Then he looked at Cal, and his eyes hardened. "Now, you!" he grated. "You horse-beater . . . listen to me, and listen close!" His stern gaze swept the group. "The horse don't live that can't be tamed without beating. This goes for all of you. The next time I see a man beating up a horse, *I'll kill him!*"

He went up to the gray, slid his hand along the quivering shoulder, smoothed its neck, caressed its jaw. And all the while he talked to it in a smiling, intimate way.

The horse, snuffing and blowing a little at the blood on Mason's shirt, quieted, nevertheless. One could see the way his tense nerves and muscles relaxed under the voice and touch.

"Now saddle him up, and do it like you know he's got more sense than you have," Mason said coldly to Cal, and walked away. But he watched over his shoulder until he saw that Cal was saddling the gray as peaceably as possible — they all noticed that.

The effect of that fight upon the Flying U outfit was not conspicuous. No one said much about it one way or the other, but a close observer would have noticed that whenever Mason was in their immediate vicinity, men with short tempers refrained from lifting booted toe to a horse's paunch when they were struggling to get the saddle cinched, that clubs were out of fashion, and that savage jerking on the bit was taboo.

One other change was apparent. Cal Emmett no longer paid any attention to Bird, although before the fight it had tickled him to have the horse come up and daintily lift a front hoof, wanting to shake hands. Whenever that happened now, he would hunch his shoulders and walk away scowling.

Things went on this way through the remainder of the beef roundup. The time for calf weaning came, and the Flying U roundup was slowly working toward the home ranch, holding what cows and calves they had gathered. Weary and Jim Mason were on day herd one day and out a mile or so from camp, when a horseman came galloping out toward the herd.

Mason and Weary had halted close together for a smoke and a lazy chat.

"Rides like Chip," Weary observed curiously when the horseman dipped into a shallow gully, galloped out of it, and then came thundering toward them. "Wonder what's up?"

Mason said nothing at all, but his face changed — became harder, with the muscles lumped along his jaw.

Chip pulled up and swung off alongside Mason. "Get on this horse of mine and pull out . . . quick as the Lord'll let yuh, Mase," he said tensely. "This is Jeff, my own horse, and here's a bill o' sale I took time to write out for yuh. Weary, you sign as witness."

Mason made no move to dismount. His mouth tightened. "Why?" he demanded. "What's up?"

Chip swallowed dryly. "Why . . . they've come after you, Mase. You and Bird. Stock inspector . . . or maybe he's the sheriff . . . and your brother-in-law. J.G.'s talking to them. I heard him tell them you'd be in off day herd in an hour. They were eating when I made a sneak out to the remuda with all your stuff I could get hold of, and a little grub, and what money I've got." He had hooked a stirrup over the saddle horn and was loosening the knot of his latigo with fingers made clumsy by his anxiety. "You can get an hour's start, if you hurry," he added.

"So Bill Crowley trailed me, did he?" Mason glanced, hard-eyed, toward camp. "Wonder how he located me away off up here?" For the first time he seemed to notice what Chip was doing. "You needn't unsaddle, Chip. I don't think I'll need your horse."

"The hell you won't!" Chip cried hotly. "You aren't going to the pen just to please that big-mouthed. . . ."

"No. But I don't want to take your horse, either."

153

"Ah . . . don't be a damned chump!" Chip protested. "I wouldn't ride Jeff once a year, anyway. Pull your saddle, Mase. You're just killing time!"

Weary looked from one to the other. "Mind telling a fella what it's all about?" he asked mildly, as Mason reluctantly dismounted.

Mason looked up at him. "Horse stealing," he said shortly, meeting Weary's amazed stare with a level-eyed glance. "I just don't happen to have the papers for Bird, that's all. He belongs to my brother-in-law."

"Mamma!" gasped Weary under his breath. "Well if that's the case, you sure better drift, 'cause there's a snaky bunch of law officers in this county, once they get after a man."

Mason uncinched his saddle, carried it over, and set it on Chip's horse, Jeff. He said nothing until he had transferred his belongings from Chip's saddle to his own and was ready to mount. "What have they done with Bird?" he asked then, looking at Chip.

"Why, they've got him tied to the bed wagon, Mase. I'd have brought him along if I'd seen any chance in the world of getting him outta camp. He's yours by rights, I

154

know that."

"You'd have a hell of a time making a jury see it that way," Mason replied stolidly. "Better go on back, Chip. I'll have to think this thing over. I don't want to mix you up in it, either one of you."

"You better do your thinking on the run, then," Chip told him restively. "I know how you feel . . . I've got horses of my own. But there ain't a chance in the world of getting Bird now. They're making damned sure of that."

Mason turned his eyes to the west where the sky was all crimson and purple with the sunset. He drew a deep, slow breath and exhaled it, then clamped his mouth shut. He looked at the two, and looked away again.

"Bill Crowley," he said between his teeth. "He hates me and I hate him. I tried my damnedest to buy Bird off him. I offered him four times what the horse was worth. But no . . . just because I loved the horse, he hung on like grim death. Rode the heart out of him. Cut him in ribbons with the spurs, beat him over the head. He used to ride him to town and leave him stand all night in the cold, and then fight him all the way home and throw him in the corral without feed and water. Part the hair on his flanks and you can feel Bill Crowley's spur marks now.

"Steal him? Of course, I stole him! What I'd ought to've done was kill the guy first. I didn't, on my sister's account. For some fool woman's reason . . . or without no reason at all, I guess . . . she claimed she loved Bill." He turned with a severe abruptness to Chip and Weary. "Who put 'em on my trail? Have you been blabbing?" His eyes bored into Chip's.

"You know I didn't. Here's thirty dollars. . . ."

"No! I. . . ."

"You damn' fool!" cried Chip. "Any of us would do this much for Bird. Make your getaway and grab the horse again when you get the chance."

Mason looked at him, shook his head. "There'll never be another chance," he said with bitterness. "Bill Crowley'll see to that."

"You better go, Mase. There ain't much time."

Mason smiled queerly. "Yes, I guess I better, Chip." He touched Jeff gently with his spurs and started off at a sharp canter. "Much obliged, kid, for all you've done!" he called over his shoulder. "I'll square it someday."

"Now what's he heading toward camp

for?" Chip worried. "He acts plumb locoed to me."

"Yeah . . . and here's that bill o' sale he forgot," said Weary. "There comes the relief. We better go overhaul Mason, don't yuh think?"

They spurred after him, and presently overtook him. Mason did not seem to be in the least locoed. From the set of his jaw and the glitter in his eyes, he seemed bent upon some grim errand that no argument could turn aside.

He took the bill of sale and put it away in an inside coat pocket while he rode. "Thanks," he said absently. "I've got wages enough coming to pay for the horse, and more. You collect the money and keep it."

"I will, if you'll take this money."

"Oh, all right. Thanks." He tucked the bills into a pocket. "Your gun's the same as mine. Got any spare shells you could let me have?"

Chip pushed a dozen or more cartridges from the little loops in his belt, and held them out to Mason. "You aren't thinking of killing off your brother-in-law and the sheriff, are you?" he questioned disapprovingly. "J.G.'d help yuh out, if he could, but he never would stand for anything like that, Mase." Chip looked at Weary.

157

"Thanks!" Mason said dryly, shoving the cartridges into the empty spaces on his own belt. "It's always handy to know all these things."

Chip twitched his shoulders impatiently. "Well, you're a damned chump to ride in and give yourself up," he said morosely. "I took a long chance, old-timer, helping your getaway. I sure wish you'd turn around and ride the other way."

"Thanks," said Mason for the third time. "You boys got any smoking material you can let me have . . . and matches?" Then, meeting the bewilderment in Chip's eyes, he added: "Keep your shirt on, kid! I'm not aiming to walk up and hold out my hands for the bracelets."

Hastily they emptied their pockets of tobacco, papers, and matches, and handed them over. Mason was setting a slow but determined pace.

Chip's worry grew unbearable. "Look here, Mase," he burst out at last, "you can't get Bird outta camp! He's tied to a hind wheel of the bed wagon, right alongside the tent. You wouldn't have a chance on earth. They'd kill yuh."

Irritation seized Mason. "I wish you'd quit beefing around about it," he snapped. "I know what I'm going to do . . . and all hell can't stop me!"

"Oh, if that's the way you feel about it!" growled Chip, and let that end it.

Mason rode with his gaze fixed straight ahead, guiding his horse mechanically around the half-sunken boulders that dotted the bald upland. Chip, stealing a sidewise glance at him, saw his teeth go hard together, but the *click* of them was lost beneath the whispery *creak* of saddle leather and the *thud* of the horses' hoofs upon the gravelly soil. Bitter thoughts darkened the mask of his face, pulled down the corners of his mouth.

Chip shuddered in spite of himself. He was young and he had not steeled himself to witness a murder unmoved.

They dipped into a long, winding coulée that opened to the badlands next to the river. Night shadows flowed up to meet them as they descended into the small walled valley.

Mason peered down ahead to the coulée's bottom, twitched the reins, and rode down the deep-worn cow trail at a shuffling trot. Dark little gullies, rock-rimmed and strewn thickly with piled boulders, wound crazily back into the hills. It soon occurred to Chip that a man might hide himself here for days, if he were afoot, or might work his way into the Little Rockies on horseback, and so defy pursuit indefinitely.

It would seem as though Mason himself were weighing the chances, for, as he rode past, he glanced speculatively aside into the gullies. Twice he turned in the saddle to look again, stirring Chip's blood to odd leaping. If only Mase would leave murder out of it!

They neared the mouth of the coulée, rode out upon the creek bottom near camp. Abruptly Mason pulled Jeff down to a walk, which was instantly matched by the mounts of his companions. Evidently he wanted to approach camp quietly — and Chip, who was certain that he knew why, had a horrible moment when he felt himself a murderer because he did not dash ahead and warn those two.

Chip looked across at Weary, and got no help there. Weary was holding in his horse to match the pace Mason had set, and in the twilight Weary's face told nothing. If he knew what was coming, it was evident that he did not mean to interfere. Chip shivered, opened his lips to make one more protest, then closed them without sound. Too late now. Nothing would stop what Mason meant to do.

Men were sitting on their heels in the open space before the bed tent. Two strangers stood watchfully apart from the others, talking together as they waited. Bird scented his master and nickered softly; he perked his ears toward the riders who were still invisible in the dusk, and heard a low, warbled note like the sleepy call of a night bird. Bird dropped his head suddenly to the knotted rope.

Not one of the men in camp noticed that. Bird's sleek rump was toward the group as the riders approached, and even when his master spoke behind him, Bird neither lifted his head nor gave any welcoming sign — an unheard-of indifference, had anyone present been calm enough to think of it.

"Well, if it isn't Bill Crowley himself!" Mason exclaimed with ironic cheerfulness. "Large as life and twice as ugly . . . heard you wanted to see me. That right, Sheriff?"

"That's right. You know why, I guess." The sheriff tilted his head toward the black horse still standing there with his head down, fussing with the rope. "This man wants his horse. He says you stole him. I'll have to ask you for your gun, Caplan."

"And you'll turn a good horse over to a man that'll starve him and ride him half to death, and rake him with the spurs to get more? Oh, hell, Sheriff." Mason peered squint-eyed through the growing darkness, taking a long last look at Bird. "You can't mean it. Why, that horse loves me like a baby loves its mother."

"Can't help it, Caplan. Crowley here has proved ownership . . . and law is law, remember. It ain't what the horse thinks about it . . . or what you or anybody thinks. The law says you're a horse thief, and I'll have to take you in. Drop your gun on the ground. I won't be hard on you, if you come peaceably."

"I sure hate to do it, Sheriff . . . but, as you say, law is law. No getting around that." Mason reached slowly for his gun.

His next movement was too swift for any there to see. He had pulled the gun slowly from its holster, seemed about to drop it beside his horse. Then he gave a twist of his wrist, and the sheriff's gun flew out of his hand as the bullet struck it. Another burst of orange flame in the gloom, and Bill Crowley yelled and crumpled, his right shoulder broken.

"Come on, Bird!" cried Mason, wheeling off behind the bed tent. "Let's get going!"

And Bird? He whirled and lashed out with his heels — twice — to send men tumbling over one another to get out of his way. He was off in a flash, his hoof beats sounding like the roll of a kettledrum beaten in finale.

"Get after him, you fellows!" yelled the sheriff as he bent and groped for his gun. "Whitmore, I call on you for help."

The Flying U boys ran to their horses.

"Talk about nerve!" Weary exclaimed under his breath. "My hat's off to that guy."

"Nerve when it comes to horse stealin'!" Cal Emmett sneered. "I always knew there was something scaly about him."

"Scaly, hell!" cried Shorty. "Me and Slim has knowed Mase Caplan for ten years and more. A whiter boy never lived. We knew all about this trouble . . . knew Bird could untie a rope, too. But I never thought of it tonight. He done it on signal."

"You knew!" gasped Chip. "Why, I thought. . . ."

"Yeah, we know what you thought." Shorty clapped a hand down on Chip's shoulder. "One yeep outta you, and we'd 'a' wiped the ground with yuh. You're sure all right, Chip. I saw you sneakin' Mase's stuff outta the tent. . . ."

"Say!" Jim Whitmore roared at them, leading his horse over to where they stood in a huddle. "When a law officer calls on yuh for help, dog-gone it, you fellers move!" Then he added a sentence that warmed the

163

hearts of his Happy Family. "Make a showin', anyhow!"

"You bet," Shorty said softly, and yelled with the next breath: "You fellers all crippled? Git a move on yuh!"

They mounted and went tearing off into the gloom. Out ahead, where the hill shadows lay thickest, there was no sound but the soft night breeze whispering over the grass.

# On the Middle Guard

Because the night happened to be fine and the cattle lay quietly sleeping, the night-guarding of the Four Eleven beef herd was a mere matter of form, and not the wearisome work it usually is. At least, the way Spider and Delaney went about it when they came out for middle guard, it was not particularly wearisome. They sought the nearest knoll where they could keep an eye on the herd, got off their horses, and sprawled in the ripened grass, smoked cigarettes, and told stories.

The cattle slept below them, a dark blotch of shade against the yellow moon-lightened prairie. Sometimes an animal coughed, or breathed long, deep-throated sighs of content, and slept again, and to the nostrils of the two came the peculiar animal odor of the herd. Sometimes off in the distance, a coyote paused in his wanderings to lift his pointed nose and clamor querulously at the moon. Straight over their heads it swam, a trifle past the full, a sphere caught somehow in its whirl through space and jammed out of perfect roundness. Spider said it looked as if somebody had been holding it against a grindstone to find out if it was phony, or if the gold went clear through.

He lay on his back — did Spider — with his gloved hands under his head and his knees drawn up, looking at the moon and taking solid comfort.

"When the moon gets to shining straight down like that, it always makes me remember things like they say yuh do when you're about to pass out by the water trail," he remarked. "Just cast your eye over the bunch, Delaney . . . I hate to move."

"Aw, they're all right," Delaney told him lazily. He, too, had a particularly comfortable position and hated to move. "Yuh couldn't start 'em with a six-gun tonight."

"Oh, I don't know," Spider drawled, feeling for a match. "Yuh can't always tell. Some uh the things I've been remembering could easy change your opinion. Did yuh ever live right in the middle of a popular romance . . . marked down to one forty-nine on the left-hand table as yuh go in . . . that yuh wasn't mixed up in no way yourself, Delaney? One where you was just plain audience in a reserved seat?"

"Are yuh sure you're awake?" Delaney wanted to know. "Romances on the left-hand table ain't, as a usual thing, perused from reserved seats. You've mixed your drinks wrong."

"Well, did yuh ever go up against one? Because I did once, and it's sure absorbing while it lasts. I wonder, did yuh ever know Jim Vanderson? Noisy Jim, we called him, 'cause he wouldn't talk unless he had to."

Delaney disclaimed all knowledge of the man, and Spider smiled reflectively up at the moon.

"Well, he was the romance, and he sure was on the bargain table when he first struck the Four Eleven for a job. He wasn't none wise to cow science, and he didn't look like he was a toiler . . . nor yet a real pilgrim. I remember us fellows had some trouble reading his brand right at the start. He wore good clothes, and brushed his teeth down by the creek everyday . . . first morning, he done it between breakfast and breaking camp, but he never repeated the offense which shows he learnt easy . . . and had all the earmarks uh the effete East. But he could ride pretty well, and, after he'd been with the outfit a while, he could top any horse in his string, which was all anybody could ask of him.

"I read him for a prodigal calf that had drifted off his home range, and I kinda chummed up to him, soon as I seen he didn't mean no harm, and could roll his own cigarettes. But he was mighty quiet, and kinda droopy by spells, and yuh couldn't get a word out uh him on night herd. So by all them signs and tokens, I also savvied that there was a girl tangled up somehow in the prodigal business. He wasn't the sort you would walk up to and ask, though, so I had to take it out in guessing.

"He'd been with us all through spring roundup, and it got along into shipping time, and Noisy Jim had got wised up some, but still he wasn't handing out no family history, so we don't know any more about him than when he come except that he's a damn' fine boy, all right, and we all liked him first-rate."

"I'm waiting a lot for that ninety-nine cent romance," Delaney reminded.

"You've been getting the first chapter. I was going to put in a lot uh fine touches, but I won't now. You get the last chapter without any filling. Tonight kinda put me in mind of it, only the moon wasn't doing business quite so brisk, and it had been whittled down more, and most times there was a bunch of clouds in the road so we couldn't see her. But it was a nice night, all the same. The cattle bedded down at dark and fair snored, they slept so sound.

"Do yuh mind that little flat over by Bad Medicine Spring? That round one that slopes off easy on all sides, like a pie tin turned bottom up? Well, there's where we bedded 'em down, and the outfit was camped below, right by the spring. It tastes rotten all right, but it was the best we could do. The whole country was almighty dry, I remember. Old Frog Wilson was cooking, and he made tea in a candy pail, and we drunk it that way."

"I will say that as a romancer yuh ain't a real success," Delaney complained. "Yuh keep quitting the trail and ambling off over the prairie, regardless. *I* ain't burning up with desire to know about Bad Medicine Spring, nor how it tastes. It's been my unpleasant misfortune to water there myself. And I don't give a cuss whereabouts yuh bedded the cattle down. I'm willing to believe they was somewhere around. Come back to the trail."

Spider smiled a superior smile, and emptied his lungs of smoke. "All is, yuh ain't got the artistic sense to appreciate fine local color," he retorted. "It's all necessary to the romance . . . it's scenery.

"Well, right there's where we was located, and we had eighteen hundred big, rollicky steers . . . which is also local color . . . and every darned one fat and sassy and hunting trouble. But they was sure tired, and was singing 'come, put me in my little bed' before sundown. Me and Smoky was due to stand middle guard, and, when we went out, we seen right away that things was coming easy and no singing to 'em for Little Willie. So Smoky, he beds down right away and commences to pound his ear, and tells me to call him after an hour or so and he'd give me a chance to slumber.

"Well, I rode around the herd a couple uh times for luck, and there was nothing doing, so I get off my horse and takes it easy myself. I didn't go to sleep, though. I just sat there on a rock, fanning my lungs with nicotine and thinking that a poor devil of a 'puncher sure earns any little snap like that . . . which he does, all right. Look at the nights when he's got to stand double shift in blizzards that's cruel for a sheep-herder to be out in . . . and them cold rains that comes in the fall, and times when the wind uses yuh for a colander and the bunch gets up and tries to walk into a change uh climate . . . which I don't blame 'em for doing. . . ."

"Oh, damn the local color!" Delaney muttered pensively.

Spider ignored the comment. "So, if a fellow gets a chance once in a while to set down on a rock and snort one, and think about his best girl and how he can make a play to see her again before the next dance, I say, go to it! And here's hoping the wagon boss don't ride up and catch yuh at it.

"So I was setting there absorbing comfort and moonlight, and casting my eye over the bunch now and then. Every son-of-a-gun was dreaming things, and the way they laid, and the poor light, made 'em look like a dark patch uh prairie . . . they laid so close and so still. I was just wondering if it wasn't time enough to wake Smoky up . . . and that's all uh the local color, if yuh want to know.

"All to once, I seen two little moons a-rising up over the edge uh the flat. I rubbers hard for a second, and says to myself . . . 'Now that there's a hell of a note!' Which it sure was, all right. I rubs my eyes and looks again, and there they are, large as life, coming right along toward me. I says again . . . 'You've sure got 'em, old boy,' and I wonders, kinda sickly, if an engine

171

has flew the track and come cutting across country . . . only engines never run in pairs that I ever saw.

"So . . . oh, well! You know how it feels to get in a crimp over something that you've gone up against unexpected, and that yuh can't savvy. Somehow it didn't look human to me, to have them two big eyes sliding at me though the dark, and no body, or no face, or anything else. First I tried to figure out what the dickens it was . . . but it wasn't half a minute till I was too scared to care a cuss, and the way I mounted my horse wasn't slow. I wonder why it is that a cowpuncher always wants to face whatever's coming, from his saddle? Put a horse between his legs and he's ready for any kind of deal, but catch him afoot, and he's plumb helpless. Anyway, them's my symptoms.

"So when them eyes headed for me out uh the dark, I climbs my horse first and yells to Smoky afterward. Smoky, he chokes off reluctant and sets up, and I guess them goo-goos was the first thing he seen, for he let a yell out uh him you could 'a' heard a mile, and the hull bunch lifted up on their feet at once. Smoky hops on his horse and lights out . . . and to hell with the stirrups! He never knowed he had any.

"I was riding Mascot that night, and

things didn't look a bit good to him, neither. He was all for burning a streak in the atmosphere, same as Smoky done, but I'd kinda come to and wouldn't have it that way. Recollect I was straddling a horse, so I wasn't feeling quite so goose-pimply, and my hat set better.

"Just then goo-goo runs foul of a big red four-year old that had been slow waking up, and he bellered a lot . . . which was some excusable . . . and the herd hit the high places. The goo-goo commenced to goggle around in a kinda wobbly half circle, and I knowed right away then what it was. It was an automobile, and it was sure on the fight. But there wasn't nothing left on that flat for it to pick a quarrel with but me and Mascot, and Mascot was trying to bluff me into thinking he wasn't scared, but just plain insulted. I'd 'a' tried to turn the bunch, but, as it was, I couldn't turn nothing but my rowels, and hang on. I did pull leather some that night, Delaney, but yuh needn't tell nobody."

"I won't," Delaney promised, "if you'll kindly tell me where the romance comes in. I've heard stampede yarns before."

"I guess yuh ain't next to romances that's handed out proper . . . they've got to be led up to gradual, which I'm doing. I ain't wise to general dispositions uh automobiles, but that one acted to me like a cayuse that's anxious to cache his head between his knees and argue with yuh some. I don't know, either, what the steer done to the internal organs uh the thing. I asked Noisy Jim, and, after he told me, I had to go off and lay down till my brain kinda settled.

"Anyway, if it hurt the automobile as bad as it had the steer, its condition must 'a' been sure serious. The excitement kinda went to its head, and it went scouring that flat looking for trouble, but there wasn't any more cattle for it to go in the air with . . . they was vanished plumb off the face uh the earth. There was just me and Mascot, and he was objecting to it.

"Well, we played tag a while, and sometimes the automobile was It, and sometimes it was us. It must uh looked some like a rough-riding contest.

"The chaffer, he hollered something at me, and it sounded kinda unpolite, only I was too busy to listen close, and it wasn't my quarrel, anyhow. Then Mascot commenced singing 'Home, Sweet Home' and hit for camp, with His Royal Goggles crowding us close. The chaffer told me afterward that he couldn't help it, and something had gone wrong with the gee-pole, but it looked to me like he done it malicious.

"We hit camp about neck and neck, and our arrival sure created a lot uh interest. Smoky had been handing it out to the boys, and they was guying him plenty about getting snakes from drinking that spring water. But when me and His Nibs bore down on 'em over the hill, they resigned and sought retirement all they could.

"Mascot turned off to the horse corral, and I got him stopped, but goo-goo goes straight ahead like it had something on its mind. First pass, it tries to walk into the bed tent, and then's when the boys scattered. You could see male humans melting away into the gloom any way you was a mind to look. There being no one to home there, it goes on over to the cook tent and shoves its nose in and says 'ka-chuckety-chuck' to old Frog Wilson. Them females . . . oh, uh course there was females . . . squawked, but it wasn't nothing to the disturbance old Frog created. He wraps himself in a dishtowel . . . which I will say wasn't no ways adequate — and it's him to the hills, yelling every jump. He acted like he'd never saw an automobile before, and, seeing this was five or six year ago, I admit they wasn't none common on the range.

"Well, goo-goo ambles clean through the cook tent, sending the stove out into the night and putting a wheel into old Frog's pan uh bread dough, and goes on a piece till it comes to them rocks piled up one side uh the spring. It climbs them a ways till it's standing on its hind legs, and got hung up on its stomach so it can't go on over. And that was sure lucky, too, for, if they'd got stacked up at the bottom uh that gully on the other side, somebody would certainly 'a' gone home in the good bye wagon.

"So there it hung, and pawed the air with its front wheels, and snorted and chuckety-chucked, but it couldn't do a blame' thing, for all it looked so hostile. The chaffer and another gazabo got down and peeled the cook tent offen the ladies, and helped 'em out. Then they pried the pan uh dough off a wheel . . . Frog was terrible sore at losing all that dough . . . and the chaffer went to tinkering with the slip-along buggy. The ladies, they set down on a rock, and the old leathery one took on something fierce, till the young one said she'd go and rustle some coffee or something to settle her nerves.

"Right there's where the romance commences, for she bumped slam into Noisy Jim. He was coming out uh the bed tent about the time they slid past, and was walk-

176

ing over to see what was up, and he fair run into the girl.

"She gave a little squeal, and says . . . 'Oh, Jim!' . . . like I'd want my girl to say it to me. And the chaffer's partner crawls out from under the devil wagon and looks at 'em a minute, and I knowed right there that it was a love story with all the fixings.

"Noisy, he acted kinda dazed, but he wasn't so far gone but he could hang onto her hands, all right, and he didn't seem to give a cuss who was looking when he gathered her to his bosom and kissed her slap on the mouth four times. I counted.

"So then they went off and set down on some rocks quite a piece from the old lady, who was still mourning for coffee . . . which she never got till breakfast time. And the chaffer and the other fellow crawled back under the automobile, and swore awful.

"Pretty soon the boys come sneaking back to camp after more clothes and an explanation, all but Frog. Him and his dishtowel stayed in the hills till the horse wrangler went out about sunup, and packed his clothes to him so he could come back and get us some breakfast.

"Well, after a while, Noisy and the girl come back looking like they'd just been to a Methodist revival and had gone forward and got religion . . . you've seen that *still* kind of look . . . and the fellow that wasn't the chaffer went off and sulked by himself, and wouldn't come when breakfast was called.

"Noisy talked the chaffer into letting him work on the automobile while the chaffer ate. I don't know what Noisy done to it. He tried to tell me afterward, but I couldn't savvy. Anyway, it wouldn't go. Us boys helped get it down off the rocks, and the chaffer turned a crank, and it just give a grunt like it was disgusted at the whole blamed business, and sulked and wouldn't answer to the rein at all.

"Uh course, then they had to stay at camp, and go on with us to Chinook. The old party rode in the mess wagon with Frog, and the chaffer and the other fellow got some grub and stayed back with the balky wagon, still doing things to it and cussing a lot. And I bet a dollar yuh can't prognosticate the end of the love tale."

"I don't want to. You go ahead . . . you're doing fine," Delaney answered.

"Well, Noisy roped a gentle old cow pony out uh his string, and had a talk with old Johnny Knott. Then he told the old party that Mildred . . . that's the girl . . . would ride a horse, instead of in the wagon. The old party objected a lot, and said things

about a riding habit, and Mildred not having any. But when she got on . . . there was
an extra saddle in the outfit that Noisy bor-
rowed, and she rode on his, which was a
peach . . . you could tell right off that she
had the riding habit, all right. She went off
as calm and easy as an old cowpuncher. But
the old lady didn't like it a bit, and Frog
said she kept asking questions about Noisy,
and handing out mean remarks about the
country.

"Us fellows had to go and hunt up the
herd, and so couldn't keep cases on Noisy
and the girl. Say! I forgot to say that girl
sure was a peach. We pulled into Chinook
and got the herd in the stockyards about
four o'clock, and rode over to camp for supper. Noisy and his girl had just rode up to
camp when we got there, and oh, doctor!
But there was a fine row going on.

"First I heard was the girl talking up to
the old woman. 'But we're married, Mama!'
she says, calm as anything. 'There's no use
making a scene now. We've been married
three hours, and I'm of age and of sound
mind, and so is Jim. You can't do anything
now but be nice about it.'

"But Mama wouldn't lay down her hand.
She seemed to want to call for a new deck
and go on playing, even if her chips *was* all

179

on the wrong side uh the table. She didn't have sense enough to pull out uh the game. She said a lot, and there wasn't none of it that Noisy needed to feel flattered over.

"Missus Noisy tried to choke her off, and finally she said to Mama . . . 'Well, we're married, and I'm very happy, and hoping you was the same,' or something like that. 'And,' she says, 'I'm going to live out here in the West with Jim, and I don't care if he *is* poor. There's worse things than marrying a poor man . . . marrying Mace Wildermere, for instance.'

"So that kinda settled the old lady, and she went off to a hotel, walking so straight her back was bent the other way, to wait for the automobile to pull into town. And Noisy and the missus went to another hotel, and, soon as they could rustle the furniture, they went to keeping house right in Chinook. They've got two kids now, and he's running the Triangle V. And I call that a romance."

# THE TALE OF A NATIVE SON

The Happy Family, waiting for the Sunday supper call, were grouped around the open door of the bunkhouse gossiping idly of things purely local when the Old Man returned from the Stock Association at Helena. Beside him on the buggy seat sat a stranger. The Old Man pulled up at the bunkhouse, the stranger sprang out over the wheel with the agility that bespoke youthful muscles, and the Old Man introduced him with a quirk of the lips:

"This is Mister Mig-u-el Rapponi, boys . . . a peeler straight from the Golden Gate. Throw out your war bag and make yourself to home, Mig-u-el . . . some of the boys'll show you where to bed down."

The Old Man drove on to the house with his own luggage, and Happy Jack followed to take charge of the team, but the remainder of the Happy Family unobtrusively took the measure of the foreign element. Their

181

critical eyes swept in swift, appraising glances from his black-and-white horsehair hatband with tassels that swept to the very edge of his gray hat, to the crimson silk neckerchief draped over the pale blue bosom of his shirt, from the beautifully stamped leather cuffs down to the exaggerated height of his tan boot heels. Unanimous disapproval was the result. The Happy Family had themselves an eye to picturesque garb upon occasion, but this surpassed even Pink's love of display.

"He's some gaudy to look at," Irish murmured under his breath to Cal Emmett.

"All he lacks is a spotlight and a brass band," Cal returned, in much the same tone with which a woman remarks upon last season's hat on the head of a rival. Miguel was not embarrassed by the inspection. He was tall, straight, and swarthily handsome, and he stood with the complacence of a stage favorite waiting for the applause to cease so that he might speak his first lines; while he waited, he sifted tobacco into a cigarette paper daintily, with his little finger extended. There was a ring upon that finger, a ring with a moonstone setting as large and round as the eye of a startled cat, and the Happy Family caught the pale gleam of it and drew a long breath. He lighted a match nonchalantly by the artfully simple method of pinching the head of it with his fingernails, leaned negligently against the wall of the bunkhouse, and regarded the group incuriously while he smoked.

"Any pretty girls up this way?" he inquired languidly after a moment, fanning a thin smoke cloud from before his face while he spoke.

The Happy Family went prickly hot. The girls in that neighborhood were held in esteem, and there was that in his tone that gave offense.

"Sure, there's pretty girls here!" Big Medicine snapped.

Miguel examined the end of his cigarette and gave a lift of shoulder that might mean anything or nothing, and so was irritating to a degree. He did not pursue the subject further, and several belated retorts were left futilely tickling the tongues of the Happy Family, which does not make for amiability.

In spite of their easy friendliness with mankind in general, they liked the new man little. At supper they talked with him perfunctorily, and covertly sneered because he sprinkled his food liberally with cayenne and his speech with Spanish words pronounced with soft, slurred vowels that made them sound unfamiliar, against which his

English contrasted sharply with its crisp, American enunciation. He met their infrequent glances with the cool stare of absolute indifference to their opinion of him, and endured their careful civility with introspective calm.

The next morning when there was riding to be done and Miguel appeared at the last moment in his work clothes, even Weary, the sunny-hearted, had an unmistakable curl to his lip after the first glance.

Miguel wore the hatband, the crimson kerchief tied loosely with the point draped over his chest, the stamped leather cuffs and tan boots with the highest heels ever built by the cobbler craft. Also, the lower half of him was encased in chaps the like of which had never before been brought into Flying U coulée. Black angora chaps they were — long-haired, crinkly to the very hide, with three white, diamond-shaped patches running down each leg of them, and with the leather waistband stamped elaborately to match the cuffs. The bands of his spurs were two inches wide and inlaid to the edge with beaten silver, and each *concha* was engraved to represent a large wild rose with a golden center. A dollar laid upon the rowels would have left a fringe of prongs all around.

He bent over his sacked riding outfit and

undid it, revealing a wonderful saddle of stamped leather inlaid on skirt and cantle with more beaten silver. He straightened the skirts, carefully ignoring the glances thrown in his direction, and swore softly to himself when he saw where the leather had been scratched through the canvas wrappings and the end of the silver scroll was ripped up. He drew out his bridle and shook it into shape, and the silver mountings and the reins of braided leather with horsehair tassels made Happy Jack's eyes greedy with desire. Miguel's saddle blanket was a scarlet Navajo, and his rope a rawhide lariat. He drew Banjo, a scruffy but reliable horse, for the day's work.

Altogether, the man's splendor when he was mounted on poor Banjo so disturbed the fine mental poise of the Happy Family that they left him jingling richly off by himself, while they rode closely grouped, and discussed him acrimoniously.

"By gosh, a man might do worse than locate that Native Son for a silver mine," Cal began, eyeing the interloper scornfully. "It's plumb wicked to ride around with all that wealth and fussy stuff. He must 'a' robbed a bank and put all the money into a riding outfit."

"And I'll gamble that's a spot higher than

he stacks up in the cow game," Pink observed. "You mind him asking about bad horses, last night? That Lizzie-boy never *saw* a bad horse . . . they don't grow 'em where he come from. What they don't know about riding they make up for with a swell rig. . . ."

"And, oh, mamma! It sure *is* a swell rig!" Weary paid generous tribute. "Only I will say old Banjo reminds me of an Irish cook rigged out in silk and diamonds. That outfit on Glory, now. . . ." He sighed enviously.

"Well, I've gone up against a few real ones in my long and varied career," Irish remarked reminiscently, "and I've noticed that a hoss never has any respect or admiration for a swell rig. When he gets real busy, it ain't the silver filigree stuff that's going to help you hold connections with your saddle, and a silver-mounted bridle-bit ain't a darned bit better than a plain one."

"Just take a look at him!" cried Pink, with intense disgust. "Ambling off there so the sun can strike all that silver and bounce back in our eyes. And that braided lariat . . . I'd sure love to see the pieces if he ever tries to anchor anything bigger than a yearling!"

"Why, you don't think for a minute he could ever get out and rope anything, do yuh?" Irish laughed. "That there Native Son throws on a-w-l-together too much dog to really get out and *do* anything."

"Aw," fleered Happy Jack, "he ain't any Natiff Son. He's a dago!"

"He's got the earmarks uh both," Big Medicine stated authoritatively. "I know 'em, by cripes, and I know their ways." He jerked his thumb toward the dazzling Miguel. "I can tell yuh the kinda cowpuncher he is . . . I've saw 'em workin' at it. *Haw-haw-haw!* They'll start out to move ten or a dozen head uh tame old cows from one field to another, and there'll be six or eight fellers rigged up like this here tray spot, ridin' along important as hell, drivin' them few cows down a *lane* with peach trees on both sides, by cripes, jingling their big silver spurs, all wearin' fancy chaps to ride four or five miles down the road. Honest to grandma, they call that punchin' cows! Oh, he's a Native Son, all right. I've saw lots of 'em, only I never saw one so far away from the Promised Land before. That there looks queer to me. Native Sons . . . the real ones, like him . . . are as scarce outside Californy as buffalo are right here in this coulée."

"That's the way they do it, all right," Irish agreed. "And then they'll have a rodeo. . . ."

*"Haw-haw-haw!"* Big Medicine interrupted, and took up the tale that might have been entitled "Some Cowpunching I Have Seen".

187

"They have them rodeos on a Sunday, mostly, and they invite everybody to it, like it was a picnic. And there'll be two or three fellers to every calf, all lit up like Mig-u-el over there, in chaps and silver fixin's, fussin' around on *horseback* in a *corral,* and every feller trying to pile his rope on the same calf, by cripes! They stretch 'em out with two ropes . . . *calves,* remember! Little weenty fellers you could pack under one arm! Yuh can't blame 'em much. They never have more'n thirty or forty head to brand at a time, and they never git more'n a taste uh real work. So they make the most uh what they git, and go in heavy on fancy outfits. And this here silver-mounted fellow thinks he's a real cowpuncher, by cripes!"

The Happy Family laughed at the idea, laughed so loud that Miguel left his lonely splendor and swung over to them, ostensibly to borrow a match. "What's the joke?" he inquired languidly, his chin thrust out and his eyes upon the match blazing at the end of his cigarette.

The Happy Family hesitated and glanced at one another.

Then Cal spoke truthfully. "You're it," he said bluntly, with a secret desire to test the temper of this dark-skinned son of the West.

Miguel darted one of his swift glances at

188

Cal, blew out his match, and threw it away. "Oh, how funny. Ha-ha." His voice was soft and absolutely expressionless, his face blank of any emotion whatever. He merely spoke the words as a machine might have done. If he had been one of them, the Happy Family would have laughed at the whimsical humor of it. As it was, they repressed the impulse, although Weary warmed toward him slightly.

"Don't you believe anything this innocent-eyed gazabo tells you, Mister Rapponi," he warned amiably. "He's known to be a liar."

"That's funny, too. Ha-ha some more." Miguel permitted a thin ribbon of smoke to slide from between his lips, and gazed off to the crinkled line of hills.

"Sure, it is . . . now you mention it," Weary agreed after a perceptible pause.

"How fortunate that I brought the humor to your attention," drawled Miguel in the same expressionless tone, much as if he were reciting a text.

"Virtue is its own reward," paraphrased Pink, not stopping to see whether the statement applied to the subject.

"*Haw-haw-haw!*" roared Big Medicine, quite as irrelevantly.

"He-he-he," supplemented the silver-trimmed one.

Big Medicine stopped laughing suddenly, reined his horse close to the other, and stared at him challengingly, with his pale, protruding eyes, while the Happy Family glanced meaningfully at one another. Big Medicine was quite as unsafe as he looked at that moment, and they wondered if the offender realized his precarious situation.

Miguel smoked with the infinite leisure that is a fine art when it is not born of genuine abstraction, and none could decide whether he was aware of the unfriendly proximity of Big Medicine. Weary was just on the point of saying something to relieve the tension, when Miguel blew the ash gently from his cigarette and spoke lazily.

"Parrots are so common out on the Coast that they use them in cheap restaurants for stew. I've often heard them gabbling together in the kettle."

The statement was so ambiguous that the Happy Family glanced at him doubtfully. Big Medicine's stare became more curious than hostile, and he permitted his horse to lag a length. It is difficult to fight absolute passivity. Then Slim, who always tramped stolidly over the flowers of sarcasm, blurted one of his unexpected retorts.

"I was just wonderin', by golly, where yuh learnt to talk!"

Miguel turned his velvet eyes sleepily toward the speaker. "From the boarders who ate those parrots, *amigo.*" He smiled serenely.

At this, Slim — once justly accused by Irish of being a "single shot" when it came to repartee — turned purple and dumb. The Happy Family, forswearing loyalty in their enjoyment of his discomfiture, grinned and left to Miguel the barren triumph of the last word.

He did not gain in popularity as the days passed. They tilted their noses at his beautiful riding gear, and would have died rather than speak of it in his presence. They never gossiped with him of horses or men or the lands he knew. They were ready to snub him at a moment's notice — and it did not lessen their dislike of him that he failed to yield them an opportunity.

It is to be hoped that he found his thoughts sufficient entertainment, since he was left to them as much as is humanly possible when half a dozen men eat and sleep and work together. It annoyed them exceedingly that Miguel did not seem to know that they held him at a distance; they objected to his manner of smoking cigarettes and staring off at the skyline as if he were alone and content with his dreams. When he did talk, they listened with an air of weary tolerance. When he did not talk, they ignored his presence, and, when he was absent, they criticized him mercilessly.

They let him ride unwarned into an adobe patch one day — at least, Big Medicine, Pink, Cal Emmett, and Irish did, for they were with him — and laughed surreptitiously together while he wallowed there and came out afoot, his horse floundering behind him, both of them mud to the ears.

"Pretty soft going, along there, ain't it?" Pink commiserated deceitfully.

"It is, kinda," Miguel responded evenly, scraping the adobe off himself and Banjo with a flat rock — and the subject was closed.

"Well, it's some relief to the eyes to have the shine taken off him, anyway," Pink observed a little guiltily afterward.

"I betcha he ain't goin' to forget that, though," Happy Jack warned when he saw the caked mud on Miguel's angora chaps and silver spurs, and the condition of his saddle. "Yuh better watch out and not turn your backs on him in the dark, none uh you guys. I betcha he packs a knife. Them kind always does."

"*Haw-haw-haw!*" bellowed Big Medicine

uproariously. "I'd love to see him git it out and try to use it, by cripes!"

"I wish Andy was here." Pink sighed. "Andy'd take the starch outta him, all right."

"Wouldn't he be pickings for old Andy, though? Gee!" Cal looked around at them, with his wide, baby-blue eyes, and laughed. "Let's kinda jolly him along, boys, till Andy gets back. It sure would be great to watch 'em. I'll bet *he* can jar the eternal calm outta that Native Son. That's what grinds me worse than his throwin' on so much dog . . . he's so blamed satisfied with himself! You snub him, and he looks at yuh as if you was his hired man . . . and then forgets all about yuh. He come outta that 'dobe like he'd been swimmin' a river on a bet, and had made good and was a hee-ro right before the ladies. Kinda 'Oh, that's nothing to what I *could* do if it was worthwhile.' "

"It wouldn't matter so much if he wasn't all front," Pink complained, "You'll notice that's always the way, though. The fellow all fussed up with silver and braided leather can't get out and *do* anything. I remember up on Milk River . . . ," and he trailed off into absorbing reminiscence, which, however, is too lengthy to repeat here.

"Say, Mig-u-el's down at the stable, sweatin' from every pore, trying to get his

saddle clean, by golly!" Slim reported cheerfully, just as Pink was relighting the cigarette
that had gone out during the big scene of
his story. "He was cussin' in Spanish, when
he seen me and got that peaceful look uh
his'n on his face. I wonder, by golly. . . ."

"Oh, shut up and go awn," Irish commanded bluntly and turned back to Pink.
"Did the fellow call it off, then? Or did you
have to wade in . . . ?"

Pink continued: "Naw, he was like this
here Native Son . . . all front. He could look
sudden death, all right . . . he had black
eyes like Mig-u-el . . . but all anyone had to
do was go after him, and he'd back up so
blamed quick. . . ."

Slim listened that far, saw that he had
interrupted a tale evidently more interesting
than anything he could say, and went off,
muttering to himself.

The next morning, which was Sunday, the
cachinnations of Big Medicine took Pink
down to the creek behind the bunkhouse.
"What's hurtin' yuh?" he asked curiously,
when he came to where Big Medicine stood
in the fringe of willows, choking between
his spasms of mirth.

*"Haw-haw-haw!"* roared Big Medicine, and,
seizing Pink's arm in a gorilla-like grip, he

194

pointed down the bank.

Miguel, seated upon a convenient rock in a sunny spot, was painstakingly combing out the tangled hair of his chaps, which he had washed quite carefully not long before, as the cake of soap beside him testified.

"Combin' . . . *combin'* . . . his *chaps,* by cripes!" Big Medicine gasped, and waggled his finger at the spectacle. *"Haw-haw-haw! C-combin'* . . . his . . . *chaps!"*

Miguel glanced up at them as impersonally as if they were two cackling hens, rather than derisive humans, then bent his head over a stubborn knot and whistled "La Paloma" softly while he coaxed out the tangle.

Pink's eyes widened as he looked, but he did not say anything. He backed up the path and went thoughtfully to the corrals, leaving Big Medicine to follow or not, as he chose.

"Combin' . . . his *chaps,* by cripes!" came rumbling behind him. Pink turned.

"Say! Don't make so much noise about it," he advised guardedly. "I've got an idea."

"Yuh want to hog-tie it, then," Big Medicine retorted, resentful because Pink seemed not to grasp the full humor of the thing. "Idees sure seems to be skurce in this outfit . . . or that there lily-uh-the-valley couldn't set and comb no chaps in broad daylight, by cripes . . . not and get off with it."

"He's an ornament to the Flying U," Pink stated dreamily. "Us boneheads don't appreciate him, is all that ails us. What we ought to do is . . . help him be as pretty as he wants to be, and. . . ."

"Looky here, little one." Big Medicine hurried his steps until he was close alongside. "I wouldn't give a punched nickel for a four-horse load uh them idees, and that's the truth." He passed Pink and went on ahead, disgust in every line of his square-shouldered figure. "Combin' his *chaps,* by cripes!" he snorted again, and straightway told the tale profanely to his fellows, who laughed until they were weak and watery-eyed as they listened.

Afterward, because Pink implored them and made a mystery of it, they invited Miguel to take a hand in a long-winded game — rather a series of games — of seven-up, while his chaps hung to dry upon a willow by the creekbank — or so he believed.

The chaps, however, were up in the White House kitchen, where were also the reek of scorched hair and the laughing expostulations of the Little Doctor and the boyish titter of Pink and Irish, who were curling laboriously the chaps of Miguel with the curling tongs of the Little Doctor, and those of the Countess, besides.

"It's a shame, and I just hope Miguel thrashes you both for it," the Little Doctor told them more than once, but she laughed, nevertheless, and showed Pink how to give the twist that made of each lock a corkscrew ringlet. The Countess stopped with her dishcloth dangling from one red, bony hand, while she looked at the results.

"You boys couldn't sleep nights if you didn't pester the life outta somebody," she scolded. "Seems to me I'd frizz them diamonds, if I was goin' to be mean enough to do anything."

"You would, eh?" Pink glanced up at her and dimpled. "I'll find you a rich husband to pay for that." He straightway proceeded to frizz the diamonds of white.

"Why don't you have a strip of ringlets down each leg, with tight little curls between?" suggested the Little Doctor, not to be outdone by any other woman.

"Correct you are," praised Irish.

"And, remember, you're not heating branding irons, mister man," she added. "You'll burn all the hair off, if you let the tongs get red-hot. Just so they'll sizzle . . . I've told you five times already." She picked up the toddler everyone called the Kid, kissed many times the finger he held up for sympathy — the finger with which he had touched the tongs as Pink was putting them back into the grate of the kitchen stove — and spoke again to ease her conscience. "I think it's awfully mean of you to do it. Miguel ought to thrash you both."

"We're dead willing to let him try, Missus Chip. We know it's mean. We're real ashamed of ourselves." Irish tested his tongs as he had been told to do. "But we'd rather be ashamed than good, any old time."

The Little Doctor giggled behind the Kid's tousled curls, and reached out a slim hand once more to give Pink's tongs the expert twist he was trying awkwardly to learn. "I'm sorry for Miguel . . . he's got lovely eyes, anyway."

"Yes, ain't he?" Pink looked up briefly from his task. "How's your leg, Irish? Mine's done."

"Seems to me I'd make a deep border of them corkscrew curls all around the bottoms, if I was doin' it," said the Countess peevishly, from the kitchen sink. "If I was that dago, I'd murder the hull outfit . . . I never did see a body so hectored in my life . . . and him not ever ketchin' on. He must be plumb simple-minded."

When the curling was done to the hilarious satisfaction of Irish and Pink, and while Pink was dancing in them to show them off, another entered with mail from town. And because the mail-bearer was Andy Green himself back from a winter's journeying, Cal, Happy Jack, and Slim followed closely behind, talking all at once in their joy at beholding the man they loved well and also hated occasionally. Andy delivered the mail into the hands of the Little Doctor, pinched the Kid's cheek, and said how he had grown good-looking as his mother, almost. He spoke a cheerful howdy to the Countess, and turned to shake hands with Pink. It was then that the honest, gray eyes of his widened with amazement.

"Well, by golly!" gasped Slim, goggling at the chaps of Miguel.

"That there Natiff Son'll just about kill yuh for that," warned Happy Jack as mournfully as he might while laughing. "He'll knife yuh, sure."

Andy, demanding the meaning of it all, learned about Miguel Rapponi from the viewpoint of the Happy Family. At least, he learned as much as it was politic to tell in the presence of the Little Doctor, and afterward, while Pink was putting the chaps back upon the willow where Miguel had left them, Pink said that the boys looked to him, Andy Green, for assistance.

"Oh, gosh! You don't want to depend on *me,* Pink," Andy expostulated modestly. "I can't think of anything . . . and, besides, I've reformed. I don't know as it's any compliment to me, by gracious . . . being told soon as I land that I'm expected to lie to a perfect stranger."

"You come on down to the stable and take a look at his saddle and bridle," urged Cal, "and wait till you see him smoking and looking past *you,* as if you was an ornery little peak that didn't do nothing but obstruct the scenery. I've seen mean cusses . . . lots of 'em . . . and I've seen men that was stuck on themselves. But I never. . . ."

"Come outta that 'dobe," Pink interrupted, "mud to his eyebrows, just about. And he knew darned well we headed him in there deliberate. And when I remarks it's soft going, he says . . . 'It *is,* kinda.' . . . just like that." Pink managed to imitate the languid tone of Miguel very well. "Not another word outta him. Didn't even make him mad! He. . . ."

"Tell him about the parrots, Slim," Cal suggested soberly. But Slim only turned purple at the memory, and swore.

"Old Patsy sure has got it in for him,"

Happy Jack observed. "He asked Patsy if he ever had enchiladas. Patsy won't speak to him no more. He claims Mig-u-el insulted him. He told Mig-u-el. . . ."

"Enchiladas sure are fine eating," said Andy. "I took to 'em like a she-bear to honey, down in New Mexico this winter. Your Native Son is solid there, all right."

"Aw, gwan! He ain't solid nowhere but in the head. Maybe you'll love him to death when yuh see him . . . chances is you will, if you've took to eatin' dago grub."

Andy patted Happy Jack reassuringly on the shoulder. "Don't get excited," he soothed. "I'll put it all over the gentleman, just to show my heart's in the right place. Just this once, though . . . I've reformed. And I've got to have time to size him up. Where do you keep him when he ain't in the show window?" He swung into step with Pink. "I'll tell you the truth," Andy confided engagingly. "Any man that'll wear chaps like he's got . . . even leaving out the extra finish you fellows have given 'em . . . had ought to be taught a lesson he'll remember. He sure must be a tough proposition, if the whole bunch of yuh have had to give up on him. By gracious. . . ."

"We haven't tried to teach him anything," Pink defended. "It kinda looked to us as if he was aiming to make us guy him, so we didn't. We've left him strictly alone. Today" — he glanced over his shoulder to where the becurled chaps swung comically from the willow branch — "today's the first time anybody's made a move. Unless," he added as an afterthought, "you count yesterday in the 'dobe patch . . . and even then we didn't tell him to ride into it . . . we just let him do it."

"And kinda herded him over toward it," Cal amended slyly.

"Can he ride?" asked Andy, going straight to the main point in the mind of a cowpuncher.

"W-e-ell . . . he hasn't been piled, so far. But, then," Pink qualified hastily, "he hasn't topped anything worse than Crow-Hop. *He* ain't hard to ride. Happy Jack could do it."

"Aw, I'm gittin' good and sick of hearin' that there tune," Happy growled indignantly. "Why don't you point out Slim as the limit once in a while?"

"Come on down to the stable, and let's talk it over," Andy suggested, and led the way. "What's his style, anyway? Mouthy, or what?"

With four willing tongues to enlighten him, it would be strange, indeed, if one so acute as Andy Green failed at last to have a very fair mental picture of Miguel. He gazed thoughtfully at his boots, laughed suddenly, and slapped Irish quite painfully upon the back.

"Come on up and introduce me, boys," he said. "We'll make this Native Son so hungry for home . . . you watch me put it on the gentleman. Only it does seem a shame to do it."

"No, it ain't. If you'd been around him for two weeks, you'd want to kill him just to make him take notice," Irish assured him.

"What gets me," Andy mused, "is why you fellows come crying to me for help. I should think the bunch of you ought to be able to handle one lone Native Son."

"Aw, you're the biggest liar and faker in the bunch, is why," Happy Jack blurted.

"Oh, I see." Andy hummed a little tune and pushed his hands deeply into his pockets, and at the corners of his lips there flickered a smile.

The Native Son sat with his hat tilted slightly back upon his head and a cigarette between his lips, and was reaching lazily for the trick that won the fourth game, when the group invaded the bunkhouse. He looked up indifferently, swept Andy's face and figure with a glance too impersonal to hold even a shade of curiosity, and began rapidly shuffling his cards to count the points he had made.

Andy stopped short just inside the door and stared, hard, at Miguel, who gave no sign. Andy turned his honest gray eyes upon Pink and Irish accusingly — whereat they wondered greatly.

"Your deal . . . if you want to play," drawled Miguel, and shoved his cards toward Big Medicine. But the boys were already uptilting chairs to grasp more quickly the outstretched hand of the prodigal, so that Miguel gathered up the cards, evened their edges mechanically, and deigned another glance at this stranger who was being welcomed so vociferously. Also he sighed a bit — for even a languid-eyed stoic of a Native Son may feel the twinge of loneliness. Andy shook hands all round, swore amiably at Weary, and advanced finally upon Miguel.

"You don't know me from Adam's off ox," he began genially, "but I know you, all right, all right. I hollered my head off with the rest of 'em when you played merry hell in that bullring, last Christmas. Also, I was part of your bodyguard, when them greasers were trying to tickle you in the ribs with their knives in that dark alley. Shake, old-timer! You done yourself proud, and I'm glad to know yuh!"

Miguel, for the first time in two weeks, permitted himself the luxury of an expressive countenance. He gave Andy Green one quick, grateful look — and a smile, the like of which made the Happy Family quiver inwardly with instinctive sympathy.

"So you were there too, eh?" Miguel exclaimed softly, and rose to greet him. "And that scrap in the alley . . . we sure had a hell of a time there for a few minutes, didn't we? Are you that tall fellow who kicked that squint-eyed greaser in the stomach? *Muchas gracias, señor.* They were piling on me three deep right then, and I always believed they'd have got me, only for a tall *vaquero* I couldn't locate afterward." He smiled again that wonderful smile, which lighted the darkness of his eyes as with a flame, and murmured a sentence or two in Spanish.

"Did you get the spurs me and my friends sent you afterward?" asked Andy eagerly. "We heard about the Arizona boys giving you the saddle . . . and we raked high and low for them spurs. And, by gracious, they were beauts, too . . . did yuh get 'em?"

"I wear them every day I ride," answered Miguel, a peculiar, caressing note in his voice.

"I didn't know . . . we heard you had disappeared off the earth. Why. . . ."

Miguel laughed outright. "To fight a bull with bare hands is one thing, *amigo*," he said. "To take a chance on getting a knife stuck in your back is another. Those Mexicans . . . they don't love the man who crosses the river and makes of their bullfights a plaything."

"That's right, only I thought, you being a. . . ."

"Not a Mexican." Miguel's voice sharpened a trifle. "My father was Spanish, yes. My mother" — his eyes flashed briefly at the faces of the gaping Happy Family — "my mother was born in Ireland."

"And that sure makes a hard combination to beat!" cried Andy heartily. He looked at the others — at all, that is, save Pink and Irish, who had disappeared. "Well, boys, I never thought I'd come home and find. . . ."

"Miguel Rapponi," supplied the Native Son quickly. "As well forget that other name. And," he added with the shrug that the Happy Family had come to hate, "as well forget the story, also. I am not hungry for the feel of a knife in my back." He smiled again engagingly at Andy Green. It was astonishing how readily that smile had sprung to life with the warmth of a little friendship, and how pleasant it was.

"Just as you say," Andy agreed, not trying to hide his admiration. "I guess nobody's got a better right to holler for silence. But . . . say, you sure delivered the goods, old boy! You must 'a' read about it, you fellows . . . about the American 'puncher that went over the line and rode one of their crack bulls all round the ring, and then. . . ."

He stopped and looked apologetically at Miguel, in whose dark eyes there flashed a warning light. "I clean forget," he confessed impulsively. "Meeting you unexpectedly like this has kinda got me rattled, I guess. But . . . I never saw yuh before in my life," he declared emphatically, following Miguel's lead. "I don't know a darn' thing about . . . anything that ever happened in an alley in the city of . . . oh, come on, old-timer . . . let's talk about the weather, or something safe!"

After that, the boys of the Flying U behaved very much as do children who have quarreled foolishly and are trying shamefacedly to reëstablish friendly relations without the preliminary indignity of open repentance. They avoided meeting the glances of Miguel, and at the same time they were plainly anxious to include him in their talk as if that had been their habit from the first. A difficult situation to meet, even with the fine aplomb of the Happy Family to ease the awkwardness.

Later Miguel went unobtrusively down to the creek after his chaps; he did not get them just then, but stood for a long time hidden behind the willow fringe, watching Pink and Irish feverishly combing out certain corkscrew ringlets, and dampening their combs in the creek to facilitate the process of straightening certain patches of rebellious frizzes. Miguel did not laugh aloud, as Big Medicine had done. He stood until he wearied of the sight, then lifted his shoulders in the gesture that may mean anything, smiled, and went his way.

Not until dusk did Andy get a private word with him. When he did find him alone, he pumped Miguel's hand up and down and afterward clutched at the manger for support, and came near strangling. Miguel leaned beside him and smiled to himself.

"Good team work, old boy," Andy gasped at length in a whisper. "Best I ever saw in m'life, impromptu on the spot, like that. I saw you had the makings in you, soon as I caught your eye. And the whole blame bunch fell for it . . . *woo-oof!*" He laid his face down again upon his folded arms and shook in all the long length of him.

"They had it coming," said Miguel softly, with a peculiar relish. "Two whole weeks, and never a friendly word from one of them . . . oh, hell!"

"I know . . . I heard it all, soon as I hit the ranch," Andy replied weakly, standing up and wiping his eyes. "I just thought I'd learn 'em a lesson . . . and the way you played up . . . say, my hat's off to *you*, all right!"

"One learns to seize opportunities without stuttering," Miguel observed calmly — and a queer look came into his eyes as they rested upon the face of Andy. "And if the chance comes, I'll do as much for you. By the way, did you see the saddle those Arizona boys sent me? It's over here. It's a pippin . . . almost as fine as the spurs, which I keep in the bunkhouse when they're not on my heels. And, if I didn't say so before, I'm sure glad to meet the man that helped me through that alley. That big, fat devil would have landed me sure, if you hadn't. . . ."

"Ah . . . *what?*" Andy leaned and peered into the face of Miguel, his jaw hanging slack. "You don't mean to tell me . . . it's true?"

"True? Why I thought you were the fellow. . . ." Miguel faced him steadily. His eyes were frankly puzzled.

"I'll tell you the truth, so help me," Andy

said heavily. "I don't know a darned thing about it, only what I read in the papers. I spent the whole winter in Colorado and Wyoming. I was just joshing the boys."

"Oh," said Miguel.

They stood there in the dusk and silence for a space, after which Andy went forth into the night to meditate upon this thing. Miguel stood and looked after him.

"He's the real goods when it comes to lying . . . but there are others," he said aloud, and smiled a peculiar smile. But for all that, he felt that he was going to like Andy very much, indeed. And since the Happy Family had shown a disposition to make him one of themselves, he knew that he was going to become quite as foolishly attached to the Flying U.

# Happy Jack, Wild Man

Happy Jack, on his way north from the Shonkin Range, saw how far it was to the river and mopped the heat-crimsoned face of his with a handkerchief not quite as clean as it might have been. He hoped that the Flying U wagons would be where he had estimated that they would be; he was weary of riding with a strange outfit where his little personal peculiarities failed to meet with that large tolerance accorded him by the Happy Family. He didn't think much of the Shonkin crew. Grangers and pilgrims, he called them disgustedly in his mind. He hoped the Old Man would not send him on that long trip with them south of the Highwoods — which is what he was on his way to find out about.

What Happy Jack *was* hoping for was to have the Old Man — as represented by Chip — send one of the boys back with him to bring over what Flying U cattle had been

211

gathered, together with Happy's bed and string of horses. Then he would ride with the Happy Family on the familiar range that was better, in his eyes, than any other range that ever lay outdoors — and the Shonkin outfit could go to hell.

He turned down the head of a coulée that promised to lead him by the most direct route — if any route in the badlands can be called direct — to the river, across which and a few miles up on Suction Creek he confidently expected to find the Flying U wagons. The coulée wound aimlessly, with precipitous sides that he could not climb even by leading his horse. Under the sweltering heat of mid-June sunlight, Happy Jack again mopped his face, more crimson than ever, and relapsed into his habitual gloom. Just when he was telling himself pessimistically that the chances were he would run slap out on a cutbank where he couldn't get down to the river at all, the coulée turned again, and showed the gray-blue water slithering coolly past the far bank, green and sloping invitingly.

The horse hurried forward at a shuffling trot and thrust his hot muzzle into the delicious coolness. Happy Jack slipped off and, lying flat on his stomach upstream from the horse, drank deep and long, then stood up, wiped his face, and considered the necessity of crossing. Just at that point the river was not as wide as in others, and for that reason the current flowed swiftly past. Not too swiftly, however, if one took certain precautions. Happy Jack measured mentally the strength of the current and the proper amount of caution that it would be expedient to use, and began his preparations. The sun was sliding downhill toward the western skyline, and he wished very much to reach the wagons in time for supper, if he could.

Standing in the shade of the coulée wall, he undressed deliberately, folding each garment methodically as he took it off. When the pile was complete down to socks and boots, he rolled it into a compact bundle and tied it firmly upon his saddle. Stranger, his horse, was a good swimmer, and always swam high out of the water. He hoped the things would not get very wet. Still, the current was strong, and his characteristic pessimism suggested that they would be soaked to the last thread. So, naked as our first ancestor, he urged his horse into the stream, and when it was too deep for kicking — Stranger was ever uncertain and not to be trusted too far — he caught him firmly by the tail and felt the current grip them both.

The feel of the water was glorious after so

long a ride in the hot sun. Happy Jack reveled in the cool swash of it up his shoulders to the back of his neck as Stranger swam out and across to the sloping green bank on the home side. Happy Jack should have sought the bottom with his feet, but the water was so deliciously cool, slapping high on his shoulders, that he still floated luxuriously — until Stranger, his footing secure, glanced back at his master sliding behind like a big red fish, snorted, and plunged onto dry land.

Then Happy Jack touched the gravelly bottom, stumbled, and let go his hold of the tail. Stranger, feeling the weight loosen suddenly, gave another plunge and went careering up the bank as he snorted again at the unrecognizable object. Happy Jack swore, waded out, and made threats, but Stranger saw himself pursued by a figure whose only resemblance to his owner lay in voice and profanity, and fled in terror.

Happy Jack crippled along painfully and fruitlessly over the stones after the horse, still shouting threats. As Stranger galloped wildly and disappeared over a ridge, Happy Jack stood and stared stupidly at the spot where the horse had been. For the moment his mind refused to grasp all the horror of his position; he stepped gingerly over the hot sand and rocks, sought the shelter of a bit of overhanging bank, and sat down dazed upon a rock too warm for comfort. He shifted uneasily to the sand, found that still hotter, and returned to the rock.

He needed to think, to grasp this disaster that had come so suddenly upon him. He looked moodily across to the southern bank, his chin sunken between moist palms, while the water dried upon his person. To be set afoot down in the badlands, away from the habitations of men and fifteen miles from the probable location of the Flying U camp, was not nice. To be set afoot *naked* — it was horrible, unbelievable. He thought of tramping barefooted and bare-legged through fifteen miles of sage-covered, rocky country with the sun beating down on his unprotected back, and groaned in anticipation. Not even his pessimism had ever pictured a thing so terrible.

He gazed at the gray-blue river that had caused this trouble that he must face and, forgetting the luxury of its coolness, cursed it venomously. Little waves washed up on the pebbly bank and glinted in the sun while they whispered mocking things to him. Happy Jack gave over swearing at the river, and turned his wrath upon Stranger, hurtling along somewhere through the breaks with all Happy's clothes tied firmly upon his back. Happy Jack sighed lugubriously when he remembered how firmly. A fleeting hope that, if he followed the trail of Stranger, he might glean a garment or two that had slipped loose, died almost before it lived. Happy Jack knew too well the kind of knots he always tied. His favorite boast, that nothing ever worked loose on his saddle, came back now to mock him with its absolute truth.

The sun, dropping a bit lower, robbed him inch by inch of the shade to which he clung foolishly. He hunched himself into as small a space as his big frame would permit, and hung his hat on his knees where they stuck out into the sunlight. It was very hot, and his position was cramped, but he would not go yet; he was still thinking — and the brain of Happy Jack worked slowly. In such an unheard-of predicament, he felt dimly that he had need of much thought.

When not even his hat could shield him from the sun's glare, he got up and went nipping awkwardly over the hot beach. He was going into the next river bottom — wherever that was — on the chance of finding a cow camp, or some cabin where he could, by some means, clothe himself. He did not like the idea of facing the Happy

Family in his present condition; he knew them too well. Perhaps he might find someone living down there next the river. He hoped so — for Happy Jack, when things were so bad they could not well be worse, was forced to give over the prediction of further evil, and pursue blindly the faintest whisper of hope. He got up on the bank where the grass was kinder to his unaccustomed feet than were the hot stones below, and hurried away with his back to the sun that scorched him cruelly.

In the next bottom — and he was long getting to it — the sagebrush grew dishearteningly thick. Happy began to be afraid of snakes. He went slowly, stepping painfully where the ground seemed smoothest; he could never walk fifteen miles in his bare feet, he owned dismally to himself. His only hope lay in getting clothes.

Halfway down to the bottom, he joyfully came upon a camp, but it had long been deserted. From the low, tumble-down corrals, and the unmistakable atmosphere of the place, Happy Jack knew it for a sheep camp, but nothing save the musty odor and the bare cabin walls seemed to have been left behind. He searched gloomily, thankful for the brief shade the cabin offered. Then, tossed up on the rafters and forgotten, he discovered a couple of dried sheep pelts, untanned and almost as stiff as shingles. Still, they were better than nothing, and he grinned in sickly fashion at the find.

Realizing in much pain that some protection for his feet was an absolute necessity, he tore a pelt in two for sandals. Much search resulted in the discovery of a bit of rotted rope, which he unraveled and thereby bound a piece of sheepskin upon each bruised foot. They were not pretty, but they answered the purpose. The other pelt he disposed of easily by tying the two front legs together around his neck, and letting the pelt hang down his back as far as it would reach.

There being nothing more that he could do in the way of self-adornment, Happy Jack went out again into the hot afternoon. At his best, Happy Jack could never truthfully be called handsome. Just now, clothed inadequately in gray Stetson hat and two meager sheepskins, he looked scarcely human. Cheered a bit, he set out sturdily over the hills toward the mouth of Suction Creek. The Happy Family would make all kinds of fools of themselves, he supposed, if he showed up like this, but he might not be obliged to appear before them in his present state of undress. He was still forced to be hopeful. He quite counted on striking some other camp before reaching the wagons of the Flying U.

The sun slid farther and farther toward the western rim of tumbled ridges as Happy Jack in his strange raiment, plodded laboriously to the north. He was forced to shift his mantle constantly into a new position as the sun's rays burned deeply, and the stiff hide galled his blistered shoulders. The sandals did better, except that the rotten strands of rope were continually wearing through on the bottom so that he must stop and tie fresh knots, or replace the bit from the scant surplus that he had prudently brought along.

Till sundown he climbed toilfully up the steep hills, and then scrambled as toilfully into the coulées, taking the straightest course he knew for the mouth of Suction Creek while he watched keenly for a white flake against green that would tell of a tent pitched there in the wilderness. He was hungry — when he forgot other discomforts long enough to think of it. Worst, perhaps, was the way in which the gaunt sagebrush scratched his unclothed legs when he was compelled to cross a patch on some coulée bottom. Happy Jack swore a great deal in those long, heat-laden hours; never did he so completely belie the name men had in sarcasm given him.

Just when he was given over to the most gloomy forebodings, a white square stood out sharply for a moment against a background of pines far below, in a coulée where the sun peered fleetingly before it dove out of sight over a hill. Happy Jack — of a truth, the most unhappy Jack one could find, although searching far and long — stood still and eyed the white patch critically. There was only the one, but another might be hidden in the trees. Still, there was no herd grazing anywhere in the coulée, and no jingle of cavvy bells came to his listening ears. He was sure that it was not the camp of the Flying U, where he would be ministered to faithfully, to be sure, yet where the ministrations would be mingled with much wit-sharpened raillery harder even to bear than was his present condition of sun blisters and scratches. He thanked the Lord in sincere if unorthodox terms, and went down the hill in long, ungraceful strides.

It was far down that hill, and it was farther across the coulée. Each step grew more wearisome to Happy Jack, unaccustomed as he was to using his own feet as a mode of travel. But away in the edge of the pine grove were food and raiment, and a shelter from the night that was creeping down on him with the hurried stealth of a mountain lion after its quarry. He shifted the sheepskin mantle for the thousandth time, then untied it from his galled shoulders and festooned it modestly if unbecomingly about his middle.

Feeling sure of the unfailing hospitality of the rangeland, whoever the tent-dweller might be, Happy Jack walked boldly through the soft spring twilight that lasts long in Montana, and up to the very door of the tent. A figure rose up — a female figure — slender, topped by a thin face and eyes sheltered behind glasses. She gazed upon him in horror, shrieked till one could hear her a mile, and fell backward into the tent. Another female figure appeared, looked, and shrieked even louder than did the first.

Happy Jack, with a squawk of dismay, turned and flew afar into the dusk. A man's voice he heard, shouting inquiry — another, shouting what from a distance sounded like threats. Happy Jack did not wait to make sure. He ran blindly until he brought up in a patch of prickly pear, at which he yelled, forgetting for the instant that he was pursued. Somehow he floundered out and away from the torture of the stinging spines, and took to the hills. A moon big as the mouth of a barrel climbed over a ridge and betrayed him to the men searching below, and they shouted and fired a gun. Happy Jack did not believe they could shoot very straight, but he was in no mood to take chances. He sought refuge among a jumble of great, gray boulders, sat himself down in the shadows, caressed gingerly the places where the prickly pear had punctured his skin — and gave himself over to riotous blasphemy.

The men below were prowling half-heartedly, it seemed to him, as if they were afraid of running upon him too suddenly. It came to him that they were afraid of him — and he grinned feebly at the joke. He had not stopped to consider his appearance, being concerned with more important matters. Now, however, as he pulled the scant covering of the pelt back over his shoulders to keep off the chill of the night, he could not wonder that the woman at the tent had fainted. Happy Jack suspected shrewdly that he could, in that rig, startle almost anyone.

He watched the coulée wistfully. They were making fires down there below him, great, revealing bonfires at intervals that would make it impossible to pass their line unseen. He could not doubt that someone was *cached* in the shadows with a gun. There were more than two men; Happy Jack thought that there must be at least four or five. He would have liked to go down just out of gun range, and shout explanations and a request for some clothes — but for the women. Happy was always ill at ease in the presence of strange women, and he felt quite unequal to the ordeal of facing those two.

He sat huddled in the shadow of a rock and wished profanely that women would stay at home and not go camping in the badlands, where their presence was distinctly inappropriate and undesirable. If the men down there were alone, he felt sure that he could make them understand. Seeing they were not alone, however, he stayed where he was and watched the fires, while his teeth chattered with cold and his stomach ached with the hunger he could not appease.

Till daylight he sat there unhappily and watched the unwinking challenge of the flames below, and miserably wished himself elsewhere. Even the jibes of the Happy Family would be endurable, so long as he had the comfort afforded by the Flying U camp — but that was miles away. Then, when daylight brought warmth and returning courage, he went so far as to wish the Flying U camp farther away than it probably was. He wanted to get somewhere and ask help from strangers rather than from those he knew best.

With that idea fixed in his mind, he got stiffly to his bruised feet, readjusted the sheepskin, and began wearily to climb higher. When the sun tinged all the hilltops golden yellow, he turned and shook his fist impotently at the camp far beneath him. Then he went on doggedly.

Standing at last on a high peak, he looked away toward the sunrise and made out a white speck on a grassy side hill; beside it, a gray square moved slowly over the green. Sheep, and a sheep camp — and Happy Jack, hater of sheep though he was, hailed the sight as a bit of rare good luck. His spirits rose immediately, and he started straight for the place.

Down in the next coulée — there were always coulées to cross, no matter in what direction one would travel — he came near running plump into three riders: Irish Mallory, and Weary, and Pink. They were riding from the direction of the camp where the women were, and they caught sight of him immediately and gave chase. Happy Jack had no mind to be rounded up by that trio; he dodged into the bushes, and, although the twigs dug long, unmerciful scratches in his person, he clung to the shelter they gave. He could hear the others shouting at one another as they galloped here and there trying to locate him, and he skulked where the bushes were deepest, like a criminal in fear of lynching.

Luck, for once, was with him, and he got out into another brush-fringed coulée without being seen, and felt himself safe for the present from that portion of the Happy Family. Thereafter he avoided religiously the higher ridges, and kept the direction more by instinct than actual knowledge. The sun grew hot again and he hurried on, shifting the sheepskin as needed.

When at last he again sighted the sheep, they were very close. Happy Jack grew cautious; he crept down upon the unsuspecting herder as stealthily as an animal hunting its breakfast. Herders sometimes carried guns — and the experience of last night burned hotly in his memory.

Slipping warily from rock to rock, he was within a dozen feet when a dog barked and betrayed his presence. The herder did not have a gun. He gave a yell of pure terror and started for camp after his weapon. Happy Jack, yelling also, followed after with long leaps. Twice the herder looked over his shoulder at the weird figure in a gray hat and flapping sheepskin, and immediately after each glance his pace increased perceptibly. Still Happy Jack, desperate beyond measure, doggedly pursued, and his long legs lessened at each jump the distance between the two. From a spectator's viewpoint, it must have been a pretty race.

With a gasp the herder dove into the tent, and into the tent Happy Jack dove after him — and none too soon. The hand of the herder had almost clasped his rifle when the weight of Happy bore him shrieking to the earthen floor.

"Aw, yuh locoed old fool, can't yuh shut up a minute?" Happy Jack had his fingers pressed against the windpipe of the other, and had the satisfaction of seeing his request granted at once. The shrieks died to mere gurgling. "What I want uh you," Happy went on crossly, "ain't your lifeblood, yuh damn' Swede idiot. I want some clothes, and some grub . . . and I want to borry that pinto I seen picketed out in the hollow down there. Now will yuh let up that yelling and act white, or must I pound some p'liteness into yuh? Say!"

"By damn, Ay tank yo' vas got soom crazy," apologized the herder humbly, sanity growing in his pale blue eyes. "Ay tank. . . ."

"Oh, I don't give a cuss what you *tank*," Happy Jack cut in. "I ain't had anything to eat sence yesterday forenoon, and I ain't had any clothes on sence yesterday, either. Send them darn' dogs back to watch your sheep, and get busy with breakfast! I've got a lot to do t'day. I've got to round up my horse and get my clothes that's tied to the saddle, and get to where I'm going. Get up, darn yuh! I ain't going to eat yuh . . . not unless you're too slow with that grub."

The herder was submissive and placating, and permitted Happy Jack to appropriate the conventional garb of a male human, while coffee and bacon maddened his hunger with their tantalizing odor. The herder seemed much more at ease once he saw that Happy Jack, properly clothed, was not particularly fearsome to look upon, and talked volubly while he got out bread and stewed prunes and boiled beans for the thrice-unexpected guest.

Happy Jack, clothed and fed, became himself again and prophesied gloomily: "The chances is, that horse uh mine'll be forty miles away and still going by this time, but, as soon as I can round him up, I'll bring your pinto back. Yuh needn't to worry none . . . I guess I got all the sense I've ever had."

227

■ ■ ■ ■

Once more astride a horse — albeit the pinto pony of a sheepherder — Happy Jack felt abundantly able to cope with the situation. He made a detour that put him far from where the three he most dreaded to meet were apt to be, and struck out at the pinto's best pace for the river and the point where he had crossed so disastrously the day before.

Having a good memory for directions and localities, he easily found the place, and, taking up Stranger's trail through the sand from there, he got the general direction of his flight, and followed vengefully after. He rode for an hour up a long grassy coulée, and came suddenly upon the fugitive feeding quietly beside a spring. The bundle of clothing was still tied firmly to the saddle, and at the sight of it the face of Happy Jack relaxed somewhat from its gloom.

When Happy rode up and cast a loop over Stranger's head, the horse nickered a bit, as if he did not much enjoy freedom while he yet bore the trappings of servitude. His submission was so instant and voluntary that Happy Jack had not the heart to do as he had threatened many times in the last few hours: to beat the hide off him. Instead, he got hastily into his clothes — quite as if he feared they might again be whisked away from him — and then rubbed forgivingly the nose of Stranger, and solicitously pulled a few strands of his forelock from under the brow band. In the heart of Happy Jack was a great peace, marred only by the physical discomforts of much sun-blister and many deep scratches.

After that he got thankfully into his own saddle and rode gladly away, leading the pinto pony behind him. He had got out of the scrape, and the Happy Family would never find it out; it was not likely that they would chance upon the Swede herder, or, if they did, that they would exchange many words with him. The Happy Family held itself physically, mentally, morally, and socially far above sheepherders — and in that lay the safety of Happy Jack.

It was nearly noon when he reached again the sheep camp, and the Swede hospitably urged him to stay and eat with him, but Happy Jack would not tarry, for he was anxious to reach the Flying U camp. A mile from the herder's camp he saw again on a distant hilltop three familiar figures. This time he did not dodge into shelter, but urged Stranger to a gallop and rode boldly toward them. They greeted him joyfully and at the tops of their voices when he came within shouting distance.

"How comes it you're riding the pinnacles over here?" Weary wanted to know as soon as he rode alongside.

"Aw, I just came over after more orders . . . hope they send somebody else over there, if they want any more repping done," Happy Jack said in his customary tone of discontent with circumstances.

"Say! Yuh didn't see anything of a wild man down next the river, did yuh?" put in Pink.

"Aw, gwan! What wild man?" Happy Jack eyed them suspiciously.

"Honest, there's a wild man ranging around here in these hills," Pink declared. "We've been mooching around all forenoon, hunting him. Got sight of him early this morning, but he got away in the brush."

Happy Jack looked guilty, and even more suspicious. Was it possible that they had recognized him?

"The way we come to hear about him," Weary explained, "we happened across some campers over in a little coulée to the west uh here. They was all worked up over him. Seems he went into camp last night, and like to scared the ladies into fits. He ain't got enough clothes on to flag an antelope, according to them, and he's about seven feet high and looks more like a missing link than a plain, ordinary man. The one that didn't faint away got the best look at him, and she's ready to take oath he ain't more'n half human. They kept fires burning all night to scare him out uh the coulée, and they're going to break camp today and hike for home. They say he give out a screech that'd put a crimp in the devil himself, and went galloping off, jumping about twenty feet at a lick. And. . . ."

"Aw, gwan!" protested Happy Jack feebly.

"So help me Josephine, it's the truth," abetted Pink, round-eyed and unmistakably in earnest. "We wouldn't uh taken much stock in it, either, only we saw him ourselves not more than two hundred yards off. He was just over the hill from the coulée where they were camped, so it's bound to be the same animal. It's a fact, he didn't have much covering . . . just something hung over his shoulders. And he was sure wild, for, soon as he seen us, he humped himself and got into the brush. We could hear him go crashing away like a whole bunch of elephants. It's a damn' shame he got away on us." Pink sighed regretfully. "We was going to rope him and put him in a cage . . . we

231

could sure've made money on him, at two bits a look."

Happy Jack continued to eye the three distrustfully. He had too often been the victim of their humor for him now to believe implicitly in their purported ignorance. It was too good to be real, it seemed to him. Still, if by any good luck it was, he hated to think what would happen if they ever found out the truth. He eased the clothing cautiously away from his smarting back, and stared hard into a coulée.

"It was likely some sheepherder gone clean nutty," mused Irish.

"Well, the most uh them wouldn't have far to go," ventured Happy Jack, thinking of the Swede.

"What we ought to do," said Pink, keen for the chase, "is for the whole bunch of us to come down here and round him up. Wonder if we couldn't talk Chip into laying off for a day or so . . . there's no herd to hold yet. I sure would like to get a good look at him."

"Somebody ought to take him in," observed Irish longingly. "He ain't safe, running around loose like that. There's no telling what he might do. The way them campers read his brand, he's plumb dangerous to meet up with alone. It's lucky you didn't run onto him, Happy."

"Well, I didn't," growled Happy Jack. "And what's more, I betcha there ain't any such person."

"Don't call us liars to our faces, Happy," Weary reproved. "We told yuh a dozen times that we saw him ourselves. Yuh might be polite enough to take our word for it."

"Aw, gwan!" Happy Jack grunted, still not quite sure of how much — or how little — they knew. While they discussed further the wild man, he watched furtively for the surreptitious lowering of eyelids that would betray their insincerity. When they appealed to him for an opinion of some phase of the subject, he answered with caution.

He tried to turn the talk to his experiences on the Shonkin range, and found the wild man cropping up with disheartening persistency. He shifted often in the saddle because of the deep sunburn that smarted continually and maddeningly. He wondered if the boys had used all of that big box of carbolic salve that used to be kept in a corner of the mess box — and was carbolic salve good for sun blisters? He told himself gloomily that if there was any of if left, and if it were good for his ailment, there wouldn't be half enough of it, anyway. He estimated unhappily that he would need about two quarts.

When they reached camp, the welcome of Happy Jack was overshadowed by the strange story of the wild man. Happy Jack, mentally and physically miserable, was forced to hear it all over again, and to listen to the excited comments of the others. He was sick of the subject. He had heard enough about the wild man, and he wished fervently that they would shut up about it. He couldn't see that it was anything to make such a fuss about, anyway. And he wished he could get his hands on that carbolic salve without having the whole bunch rubbering around and asking questions about something that was none of their business. He even wished, in that first bitter hour after he had eaten and while they were lying idly about in the shady spots, that he was back on the Shonkin range with an alien crew.

It was perhaps an hour later that Pink, always of an investigative turn of mind, came slipping quietly up through the wild rose bushes from the creek. The Happy Family, lying luxuriously on the grass, was still discussing the latest excitement. Pink watched his chance and, when none but Weary observed him, jerked his head mysteriously toward the creek.

Weary got up, yawned ostentatiously, and

sauntered away in the wake of Pink. "What's the matter, Cadwolloper?" he asked when he was close enough. "Seen a garter snake?" Pink was notoriously afraid of snakes.

"You come with me, and I'll show yuh the wild man." He grinned.

"Mama!" exclaimed Weary, and followed stealthily where Pink led.

Some distance up the creek, Pink signaled caution, and they crept forward through the grass like Indians, on hands and knees. On the edge of the high bank they stopped, and Pink pointed. Weary looked over, and came near whooping with laughter at the sight below. He gazed a minute, drew back, and put his face close to the face of Pink.

"Cadwolloper, go get the bunch!" he commanded in a whisper, and Pink, again signaling needlessly for silence, slipped hastily away from the spot.

Happy Jack, secure in the seclusion offered by the creekbank, ran his finger regretfully around the inside of the carbolic salve box, eyed the result with dissatisfaction, and applied the finger carefully to a deep cut on his knee. He had got that cut while going up the bluff just after leaving the tent with the shrieking females. He wished there was more salve, and he picked up the cover of the box and painstakingly wiped out the inside; the result was disheartening.

He examined his knee dolefully. It was beginning to look inflamed, and it was going to make him limp. He wondered if the boys would notice anything queer about his walk. If they did, there was the conventional excuse that his horse had fallen down with him — Happy Jack hoped that it would be convincing. He took up the box again and looked at the shining emptiness of it. It had been half full — not enough by a long way — and maybe someone would wonder what had become of it. Darn a bunch that always had to know everything, anyway!

Warned at last by that instinct which tells of a presence unseen, he turned around and looked up apprehensively. The Happy Family, sitting on the bank upon their heels in a row, looked down at him gravely and appreciatively.

"There's a can uh wagon dope up at camp," Cal Emmett informed him sympathetically.

"Aw . . . ," Happy Jack began, and choked upon his humiliation.

"I used to know a piece uh poetry about a fellow like Happy," Weary remarked sweetly. "It said . . . 'He raised his veil, the maid turned slowly 'round, looked at him, shrieked, and fell upon the ground.' Only in this case" — Weary smiled down upon him blandly — "Happy didn't have no veil."

"Aw, gwan!" adjured Happy Jack helplessly, and reached for his clothes, while the Happy Family chorused a demand for explanations.

# BY GOLLIES, YES!

The wind whooped over the rim rock, bellowing the arrival of a late spring storm. It ruffled the hair of the lean range cattle and sent them shivering into the scant shelter of the willow along Squaw Creek. Up that creek, *click-clack*ing over the loose rocks in the trail through the willows, rode big Bill Grimes — who men called Banty for his very bigness — singing lugubriously an old range song of many stanzas and doubtful propriety.

Across the old-fashioned narrow fork of his sun-blistered stock saddle two willow-covered demijohns hung suspended by three feet of frayed cotton rope, jogging his knees already blissfully bruised by two full gallons of whiskey nefariously peddled through a country gone dry. Behind the cantle rode a bundle of newspapers the size of his arm, and below that swung a ragged gunny sack with smoking tobacco in it, two pounds of plug, and a package of baking soda that was leaking badly at one corner.

On Banty's high cheek bones flamed the red flush of his potations; in Banty's far-sighted blue eyes flared a light that could easily grow acrimonious, although just now it was mellowed by song and the happy consciousness of those full jugs.

"Fer I'm a young cowboy an' I know I done wrong . . . ," wailed Banty after a full-flavored, improvised stanza of exploits that will never see print. "Move along there, you cow-faced, mule-eared, sheep-hided ole skate, you! We're packin' big news into camp . . . by gollies, yes! *And* whiskey. An' if we don't cache the whiskey and serve the news first, the kid ain't goin' to git the full significance of them news we're bringin' him. Serve the news an' save the whiskey . . . by gollies, yes! The kid he cain't carry his whiskey like what I kin. In all my esperances and travels I never seen no one that could." "Fer I'm a young cowboy an' I know I done wrong. . . ."

Around a bend in the trail rode he who Banty spoke of as the kid. Small he was, lean and leathery and bowlegged, with a squint to his shrewd brown eyes and a whimsical twist to his age-hardened lips. He may have lived fewer years than Banty, but

239

he did not look it. Over his shoulder he carried a long-handled irrigating shovel with fresh mud still clinging to the blade. While the horses rubbed noses together in pleased greeting, he eased the shovel to the ground and stared at the musical Banty with hard disfavor.

"Leave it to you!" he snorted. "So that's why you never showed up last night! Loaded to the guards . . . and what you couldn't pack inside you brung along in jugs! Ain't you got any sense at all, you old fool? Where's my tobacco? Forgot it, uh course!"

"Now, now, Grit, don't go gitting espenurious. I got it. I got the chewin' and the smokin' both, an' I even got the sody." Banty's tone was huskily virtuous. "An' that ain't all, Grit. I'm packin' bigger things than sody and chewin' tobacco, Grit. In all my esperances. . . ."

"You're darn' right . . . you're packin' a jag that'd kill a mule. Just when you're needed most on the ranch, too! I been up against it right, while you was tankin' up in town. One of them new Herefords is sick, and, if it ain't blackleg, then I don't know blackleg when I see it, that's all. I been tryin' to push the young stuff outta the creek bottom, and doing it alone ain't any snap the way they hang to the brush in this wind. You'd ought to've got in last night. What in Sam Hill ails yuh, Banty? Gitting drunk at a time when you're needed most . . . what in thunder made you do it?"

"Now, now, Grit, this ain't the time or the place to begrutch a man a drink er two. I rode into big news, Grit. You an' me is livin' hist'ry. By gollies, yes! Over in Yer-yerup-p!" The word came out in a hiccup that Banty tried to conceal with an immediate cough. "We're fixin' to clean up them Germans right. We're goin' over there. . . ."

"Who? You?" Grit eyed him contemptuously. "Say, Banty, for the love of Murphy, what you been drinkin?"

Banty straightened himself affrontedly. "That there's beside the point. If you had one spark of patri'sm burnin' in your soul, you wouldn't never ask what have I been drinkin', ner what has *anybody* been drinkin'. When my country calls me, Grit, am I the one to hide my head under the blankets? By gollies, *no!*" He beat his chest with his gloved fist, as he had once seen a Congressman do in a campaign speech. "When my country calls Banty Grimes, he says . . . 'Here I am, come an' git me!' "

"That's what Long Henry said when the posse got him cornered in the shack over on Forty Mile," Grit checked him bluntly.

241

"Your country ain't goin' to be out such a hell of a lot if you don't answer when she calls. Gimme them jugs. And you ride on over to the house and sober up, you danged old windbag."

Banty did not want to give up the demijohns. The light in his eyes turned crafty. He reined his horse out of the trail, meaning to pass Grit unobtrusively while he argued.

"Now, Grit, what's in them jugs ain't neither here nor there. We ain't talkin' about them jugs . . . but, seein' you mention it, I did bring out a little liquor to have in case uh sickness. Time you et them sour beans, a good shot uh whiskey would 'a' straightened you out in no time, 'sted uh sufferin' the way you done. I tuk a drink comin' out, yes. I ain't denyin' I tuk a drink. I was shore chilled to the bone, ridin' ag'in' this wind. She shore cuts up on top the ridge. In all my esperances an' travels I never seen a wind like this wind has blowed. It's jest. . . ."

"Hold on! You gimme them jugs. I'll take charge of 'em myself . . . just in case of sickness." Grit grinned shrewdly. "You can't fool me, Banty. I know to a drop how much it takes to bring out them experiences and travels of your'n. You're drunk. You know dang' well you're drunk. Hand over them jugs. You want to go and git snakes ag'in, you old fool?" He rode close, reaching for the nearest demijohn.

Banty backed his horsed precipitately. "Grit, you leave them jugs be! I'm jest as competent to take care of 'em as what you be. By gollies, yes! You'd go right to work and git drunk. I know you, Grit, a hull lot better'n what you think I know yuh. Our country's honor is at stake. The hounds of ow-tocracy is knockin' on our door, Grit. On your door an' my door. We gotta rise up an' kick 'em out. As free American citiz-z-zns."

"Aw, quit that buzzin' an' git to the house!" Grit turned and spat disgustedly into the whipping brush alongside the trail. "Keep your danged whiskey, then. But if I ketch you drinkin' any more tonight. . . ."

From the wildness of Banty's patriotism Grit guessed shrewdly the depth of his debauch. Banty was large, and, drunk or sober, he had the strength of three such men as Grit. To take the jugs by force was quite beyond Grit's physical limitations. He let Banty ride on with his demijohns and turned his mind to strategy.

When Banty was quite out of sight, Grit swung off the trail, forcing his horse through the willows to open ground beyond. By trotting briskly he passed Banty on the winding trail while the old sinner was still well hidden in the thicket, and reached the stable unseen. Hurriedly he hid his horse, Yaller, behind the butt of a haystack, and climbed stiffly into the stable loft.

Grit knew the mind of Banty, drunk or sober. He knew that the meeting down the trail had been a mischance that Banty would have given much to avoid. Banty would hide the demijohns just as surely as a hen turkey will hide her nest, nor would it be the first time that Banty had brought whiskey to the ranch and hidden it away from Grit in the vain hope that Grit would not suspect his fall from grace.

The shivering and the waiting stretched from five minutes to ten, yet Banty did not come.

"The danged old fool has fell off his horse, I bet," grumbled Grit when the ten minutes had lengthened to fifteen and the shivering had developed into a chattering of teeth. "I could crawl to where I left him and back ag'in by now. Mebby I'd oughta go look him up."

At that moment Banty appeared, riding out from the willows to the gate. As clumsily as Grit had pictured him, he dismounted and fumbled at the wire loop. Quite suddenly it slipped off the stake, the gate fell into limpness on the ground, and with it fell Banty.

Banty floundered to his knees, crawled to the fence post, and with that to steady him he got to his feet. His horse waited for his next move, decided that there would be none, and stepped cautiously over the loosened wire and waited again, tail to the wind. So much was training hardened into habit.

Banty cautiously let go the post and stooped to pick up the gate. But the wind swooped down in a heavy gust, caught him full astern just when his balance was most precarious, and sent him forward on all fours again. It was not altogether the fault of Banty's condition, but up in the stable loft Grit snorted again and cursed Banty anew for a drunken old fool, his indignation growing with the chill that searched the marrow of his bones.

Once more Banty crawled laboriously to the fence post and struggled to his loose-jointed six feet with five extra inches for good measure. "That shore is some wind," he complained. "By gollies, yes! In all my esperances and travels I never seen a wind like this here wind. Chills a feller to the bone. Takes the gimp out of a feller."

With one arm around the post to steady himself, he reached into an inside pocket and drew out a half-pint flask, nursing it affectionately between his palms, ogling it foolishly as a half-wit ogles a pretty girl. He uncorked the flask, parted his great walrus mustache, and with a smack of anticipation proceeded to replace some of that gimp that the wind had taken out of him.

All this Grit saw through the knothole, and swore again. Banty replaced the cork, pressing it tightly, resettled his ragged mustache, put the flask in his pocket, and stooped again, reaching for the gate. Once more he slipped down and then wondered why he should get up when he could lie still and save himself the jolt of another fall. One of America's free and loyal citizens was snoring when Grit came bowlegging it indignantly from the barn.

With his arms on his hips, Grit glared down at the ungainly slumbering figure sprawled across the loose wires at the fallen gate. He looked at Banty's saddle from which the two demijohns no longer swung. Banty had been more cunning than Grit had foreseen, and had hidden the whiskey somewhere along the trail.

"You shore are a sweet mess uh human failings, ain't yuh? Git up! Even a hog picks itself a hollow to lay in. It don't bed down on bob wire. Git up!" His foot went out to poke Banty in the ribs.

Grit fumbled in Banty's coat, found the flask, and refreshed himself generously. With the quick ardor of the fiery liquor he then heaved Banty off the wires and closed the gate.

Banty slept peacefully on, snoring occasionally in half-strangled snorts most unpleasant to hear. Grit tried again to rouse him with revilings, sundry mild kicks, and shakings, but Banty would not budge.

He decided to bring blankets and cover Banty from the searching cold, letting him sleep off his drunkenness where he lay. But when he had brought two heavy blankets from the cabin, he could not cover Banty. That terrific wind bellied the blankets out like sails and nearly carried Grit off his feet when he attempted to spread them. Even a rock or two placed on one corner while he essayed to anchor the other did not help much; the wind jerked them from under the rocks so that they slapped Grit spitefully and carried him down in a heap. He untangled himself and got up, lowered the amber line appreciably in the half-pint flask, and swore whistling oaths through a gap in his strong front teeth.

"By gollies, yes!" mumbled Banty between snores, whereupon Grit cursed him anew. With some effort he wadded the blankets into a bundle and threw them viciously from him into the barbed-wire fence, where they clung, flapping.

Many an emergency had Grit met and conquered with sheer nerve and a certain ingenious wit, else he would not have been there worrying over Banty that night. Since Banty must not be left outside to freeze while he slept, and since Grit could neither waken him nor carry him unawakened, he did the next best thing. He mounted Banty's horse and rode to the stable where tools of all sorts lay scattered about, unfastened Banty's rope from the saddle, looped it to the nose of an ungainly triangular stone boat that Grit succinctly termed a go-devil, and, in spite of the horse's objections, dragged it down to the gate.

He loaded Banty precariously on the contraption, heart pounding sullenly as he did so from the inert dead weight of him, and hoped Sam for once would show sense. Mounting Banty's horse, he strove again to bring home his burden.

When the go-devil finally struck a rock with such force that Banty rolled off, Grit threatened to leave him there to freeze to death. Instead, he took the horse to the corral, turned him inside, and shut the gate. Then he went wabbling around and pulled his own dun-colored cayuse away from the haystack where he was industriously feeding. Not for nothing had men dubbed Frank Bowles Grit in his youth; not for nothing did Grit cling to his horse Yaller, although the high winds of Idaho never roughened the hair of a meaner-looking beast. Yaller rolled an eye as malevolent as the eye of a hippopotamus, seized with a vicious yank a last mouthful of hay, laid back his ears, and munched sullenly while Grit mounted uncertainly. Still munching, Yaller struck his customary little racking trot, philosophically thankful that he had been left so long to eat in peace.

"You can tell a man by the horse he rides," Grit declaimed while he racked down to the gate. "Banty's been ridin' that cow-backed monstrosity for six year and more, and I'll be darned if one ain't as no-account and ornery as the other. Git 'em in a pinch and they ain't there, either one of 'em. I'll be darned if I'd own a horse that won't pull nothin' but hay out of a manger . . . I'd knock 'im in the head and haul him out fer coyote bait! But Banty, he don't know a good horse from a bad horse . . . why . . .

you Yaller! That ain't nothin' but Banty, dog-gone his ornery hide! I'd oughta be skimming the milk to feed them calves right now, 'stead of haulin' his measly carcass in like a sick cow."

Once more Grit loaded Banty on the go-devil, this time with a stumbling awkwardness quite new to him. Once more he fumbled his foot into the stirrup, crawled into the saddle, and started for the cabin. Yaller was a real rope horse. He would pull under the saddle as much as any horse his size could be expected to pull in harness. With the wind whipping his mane and blowing his tail out straight, Yaller dug in his rock-chipped hoofs and hauled Banty and the go-devil to the cabin.

At the door they stopped with a lurch, and Banty raised his head. He fumbled vaguely at his pocket, roused to grope more definitely, was shocked into full awakening by the absence of that which he sought, and sat up glaring accusingly at Grit, who had dismounted to drag his partner into the house.

"Where's my bottle?" Banty demanded with a startling coherence. "I got a chill. In case uh sickness . . . an' I'm a sick man, Grit . . . a *damn'* sick man! What you mean goin' through a man's pockets? Grit, if you've went an' took my bottle. . . ."

"Yes, darn yuh, I went and took that bottle." To prove it Grit stood there beside the go-devil and helped himself to another drink, glaring down defiantly into Banty's bloodshot, horrified eyes.

Bellowing vague anathema at the outrage, Banty clumsily heaved himself off the go-devil and made for Grit. He stubbed his toe on the crude point of his conveyance and went down, and Grit made haste to drain the flask before Banty regained a more or less precarious footing. When Banty again came lurching to the attack, Grit flung the empty bottle and caught Banty on the middle button of his vest.

"There's your dog-gone' bottle . . . take it!" Grit announced insultingly.

Banty emitted a grunt, swayed uncertainly for a minute, and rushed again, grabbing ineffectually for Grit, who with some difficulty remounted while Banty raved.

"If the milkin' was done and the calves fed, I'd lick you to a fare-you-well," Grit told Banty grimly while he flipped his rope off the go-devil and coiled it sloppily. "But I've wasted more time on yuh now than what you deserve. I'd oughta left yuh bedded down on that bob wire to freeze. You couldn't come alive and walk to the house . . . oh, no! You had to be hauled up like a sick cow. But you can come to life all right soon as you git here . . . like as if I was runnin' a dang' streetcar for yuh! Think I got nothin' to do but haul yuh around the ranch? You shore are a bird, all right!"

By that time Grit was at the corral whither Yaller had carried him while he talked. Banty was up at the cabin, weaving here and there in the windy dusk, trying to find Grit so that he could kill him, trying to find the bottle in the hope that it was not yet empty, trying to find the cabin door that he might go in and get a lantern with which to find Grit and the bottle.

Down at the corral, Grit went fumbling to his task, still haranguing the absent Banty upon the subject of his shortcomings.

The two calves were blatting insistently in a nearby shed, and Grit started for the house that he might bring down their supper. In the dark with the wind blowing a gale, he wove a strange pattern of footprints in the loose sand. Twice he veered altogether from the path and brought up against a sagebrush. Once he canted off into the woodpile, from which he retreated with much care, his whole fogged mind fixed upon saving the milk. But eventually he reached the cabin, found the door, and pushed against it, recoiled, braced himself, and pushed again, this time sliding Banty's sleeping body across the floor so that the door would open. To assist in the opening, Banty unconsciously drew up the leg that had been straight — so Grit stumbled in with the milk.

In the darkness a sober man would probably have done what Grit did. He sprawled full length over Banty, pouring what was left of the milk over Banty's head and shoulders. A sober man would have lost his temper — Grit went raving mad.

Bellowing, blinking, and sputtering milk from eyes and nostrils, Banty heaved himself up into a swirl of flailing milk bucket, flailing arms, kicking feet, and curses. He tried to grapple with Grit and put one arm around his middle. Immediately he tried to let go, to back away, to crawl under the bunk, the table, anywhere to escape. Grit was everywhere, and, wherever he was, there was tumult and distress. Banty was bigger and stronger. Like a bull with a wildcat on its withers, he then bawled in dazed terror and could not use that strength.

The bucket came down on its edge and caught him over one shaggy eyebrow, and he yelled. A boot toe came up from somewhere in the dark with a terrible impact against his left ribs, and he yodeled like a kicked pup. Whichever way he turned, there was Grit just landing a blow with hands, feet, or milk bucket.

Chance threw Banty against the doorway at last and he clawed his way to outer darkness and wind and a blessed safety. Some instinct of self-preservation sent him weaving down the path to the stable, where he groped his way to an empty stall filled with hay and burrowed deeply into it, whimpering over his hurts.

At the cabin, Grit stood braced in the doorway, shrilling raucous challenge into the windy night. Tears of anger slid down his leathery cheeks and salted his rage-twisted mouth.

The hungry bawling of the two calves, once more stirred to hope of supper by the coming of Banty, pulled Grit back to plodding sanity. He turned back into the cabin, staggered to a certain corner, and got a lantern off a nail, plucked a match out of the battered tin match safe on the wall nearby, and lighted the lantern. These things he could do in the dark, drunk or sober; ten years of hanging a lantern on a certain nail in a certain corner of a cabin and of reaching just so far in a certain direction for a match will wear deep the groove of habit in any man's brain.

The table was canted against the wall and the floor was sprinkled with unwashed dishes left over from Grit's hurried dinner. He righted the table, set an overturned chair upon its four legs, and seated himself gingerly as though he was afraid someone would attempt to pull the chair away.

"Twenty year I've stood fer Banty," he mumbled irefully. "And now look at that floor! A hul milkin' wasted on him . . . an' I hope the old tomcat freezes to death. And them calves, bawlin' their fool heads off, an' me drunk on that damn' rotgut that ain't fit fer a Piegan, let alone a white man that's got a ranch an' cattle to take care of and a measly no-account pardner that ain't worth hangin' . . . an' I hope to hell he *does* freeze!"

He wiped his eyes frankly and primitively on his sleeve, reached behind him for the coffee pot that stood on the stove, gleaned a white enameled cup from the floor, and poured it full of coffee, black and strong. Grit did not particularly care for cold coffee, but he emptied the cup deliberately, refilled it, and drank again.

As the dizzying fumes of the whiskey subsided under the sobering effect of the coffee, Grit managed to skim the morning's milk and with it stop the blatting of the calves. He unsaddled Yaller and Sam, and fed and watered them with absolute impartiality, although he loved the one and despised the other. He gathered the eggs in a battered old basin coated with bran mash long dried, and shut the chicken house against all the various night prowlers of the sage land — weasels, coyotes, bobcats, and skunks. He carried in two great armloads of wood and started a fire. That he did it with his ears keen for some sound of his erring partner he would have denied under torture.

"Let him freeze if he don't know enough to come in. Yes, dog-gone him, let him freeze and be darned to him," he muttered at intervals while he plodded about his work. "He might mebby make pretty fair kioty bait . . . I dunno. He shore ain't good fer nothin else."

By dim lantern light he filled and trimmed the lamp and wiped out the chimney that had long lacked such attention. He set the lamp on the table where its light would shine straight out through the window into the stormy darkness, then blew out and hung the lantern back in its place. Sleet was falling now, rattling on the low roof, lashing viciously against the grimy windowpanes. Grit's eyes turned often that way, and once he caught himself picturing Banty lying out somewhere in that driving gale, freezing slowly while he slept. He turned abruptly from the window.

"That heifer's dead by now, I reckon," he hastened to explain his anxiety. "I'd oughta gone down and put her out of her misery. I would 'a' done it, if it hadn't been for Banty. If he'd been here, them cattle wouldn't 'a' broke the ditch and made extra work fixin' it, and I could 'a' looked after that sick critter like I intended. I hope to hell he does freeze!"

Grit's head ached from whiskey poison, and his stomach, inclined toward dyspepsia from years of too much fat meat and hot bread and long-boiled coffee, rebelled against the thought of food. Yet he sliced salt pork, warmed the boiled beans, made twice as much fresh coffee as one man could drink, mixed sourdough biscuits, and watched them solicitously while they baked.

Finally he set down the coffee pot, went to the door, and opened it. The snow sucked in on him in gusts; the wind shrieked and whooped around the cabin's corner; the lamp flared and guttered and went out, leaving the room black, dark, and drafty.

"The darned old fool will freeze," he told himself savagely, and forced the door shut against the storm. "I'll be dog-darned if I ever seen his match for pigheadedness."

He went groping across to where he had hung the lantern on its nail, took it down again, and reached for a match. "I'd oughta go take a look at that heifer," he said — and added reluctantly: "I s'pose I'd oughta hunt Banty up. He's went and connected up with them two demijohns and he'll drink till he's plumb paralyzed. It's up to me to find him . . . but I'll be dog-darned if it don't go ag'in' the grain!"

Had Banty been there and heard him, he would have realized the extremity of emotion that Grit had reached. Like Banty and his "esperances and travels", Grit never said "dog-darned" until he had passed a certain point in his patience and his endurance. Having said it twice in as many minutes, Grit no longer pretended to himself that he did not care whether Banty froze or not. He waited only long enough to set the food in the oven where it would keep warm, and to fill the stove with wood and close the front as tightly as possible, banking a broken place with ashes to hold the fire against too fast a flame. Then bundled in his frayed sour-dough coat, he took up the lantern, and went supperless into the storm.

■ ■ ■ ■

At daylight the hay pile in the empty stall heaved with internal convulsion. A half-grown black pig emerged, grunting protest that ended in a squeal as Banty's boot caught it neatly on one rounded ham. Next came Banty, pushing the loose hay off his head and shoulders, staring with his one good eye at the dim interior of the stable with the blank gaze of the sleeper who wakens to unfamiliar surroundings. He looked at the pig, sent another kick toward it, and realized that he ached — just where he did not at first know. He lay back blinking, and tried to recall what had happened and why he was sleeping with the black shoat in the stable, instead of in his own bunk.

He sat up stiffly and felt in his pocket for the flask, found the pocket empty, and remembered vaguely how Grit had stood over him while he drained the bottle, and had flung it at him afterward. Banty had not done a thing to Grit. He distinctly remembered that he had spoken very pleasantly when they met on the trail, and the next thing he knew Grit had emptied the bottle he had stolen and thrown the flask —

witness the terrible pain in Banty's middle where the bottle had hit him. Grit was drunk — blind, raving drunk, else he never would have tried to kill Banty in the cabin for no reason at all. He must have had more whiskey than was in the flask.

"I tuk one good drink outta that bottle right there at the gate when I got that chill. The kid he must 'a' got at the jugs . . . by gollies, if the kid has got them jugs!"

He got up, groaning with the stabbing pain in his head when he moved, kicked the pig again because it looked so comfortable while he was so full of pain, and let himself out of the stable.

The cabin stood, bleak and forlorn, in the lee of a great snowdrift. Around it and over it the floury snow went whirling in a steady fog-like mass that lifted and swooped again as the wind drove it along in fresh gusts of fury. From the quivering stovepipe, well anchored but leaning drunkenly away from the storm, a thin pennant of smoke whipped raggedly to the southeast. Toward the cabin Banty labored through the snow, his weight carrying him down to his hips at every step — every step a fresh agony.

Grit was sitting hunched over the stove hearth, trying to get a little heat into his chilled body. His face was gray with exhaustion, his eyes sunken with worry, his rheumatic back racked with pain from exposure and trampling through snow. Grit was not thinking of his weariness and aching back, however. He was trying to guess just how far Banty had traveled before he stumbled and fell, and, having fallen, lay where he was and slept. Which direction had he taken?

At that point in his musings Banty pushed the door violently open and stumbled in. Grit's jaw went slack with amazement, but he made no movement toward welcome. Life had schooled Grit to hide his deeper emotions as jealously as he would have hidden a crime. Beyond a sudden trembling of his hands outstretched to the heat, and a quick breath, and the eager light in his eyes, he remained passive, neutral, until he saw what attitude Banty would assume.

Banty's attitude was speedily made manifest. "Grit, what you done with my whiskey? I'm a sick man and I need some. Dig it up, darn yuh . . . I know you've got it."

Grit leaned stiffly, pulled open the stove hearth, spat into the ashes, and carefully pushed the iron slide back until only an inch crack was left for draft. "And if I did have it, you wouldn't get any," he retorted huskily. His glance went sharply to Banty's distorted countenance, looking for signs of frostbite. That Banty had survived a night in the blizzard was incredible. That he nowhere betrayed the white signal of frost left only one explanation. Grit guessed shrewdly, and spoke his guess. "You must 'a' bedded down with the rest of the hogs last night. If you'd waited a spell, I might 'a' fed you with 'em."

"That ain't neither here nor there, where I bedded down. I shore would ruther sleep with the hogs than with a fightin' drunk pardner that tried to kill me. By gollies, yes! Hogs is white folks alongside a pardner that steals a gallon and a half . . . three quarters, fer I only took out a little better'n a quart, and you got the bulk of that. Grit, you gotta dig up that whiskey. I ain't sayin' nothing about you tryin' to murder me . . . you was drunk, and, when you're drunk, you ain't accountable. But you was drunk on my whiskey, paid for with my own money, recollect. We'll let that pass by, even if you did take it offen me. All I ask is them two jugs I brought home. I need a shot now to straighten me out. I'm willin' to forget how you come by 'em." He sat down heavily beside the stove, one knee touching Grit's knee, and waited.

"The coffee's 'most done," said Grit after

a minute. "That'll do yuh more good than whiskey."

"By gollies, Grit, when I say whiskey, I don't mean coffee! I'm sick as a dog and I know what I want to straighten me up. I'm tellin' you fair and peaceable, you'd better dig up them jugs uh mine."

Grit turned his head and stared hollow eyed at Banty. "Seems to me you're takin' a whole lot for granted, old-timer. I never said I had your whiskey. You better go kinda easy." Then he added dispassionately: "There's bread and beans and meat in the oven there. I warmed over last night's sup-per. What you want is to get yourself outside some grub."

The mere thought of grub nauseated Banty, who staggered to his bunk, mutter-ing under his breath what Grit assumed to be oaths and vague, unfinished threats. Fine snow had sifted in through the cracks around the little window beside Banty's head, so that the pillow was thinly covered as frost coats a windowpane. The chill of it was welcome to Banty, who lay face down upon it and gave himself wholly to his physi-cal ills.

Buttoned once more into his sour-dough coat with an old cap pulled down to his col-lar, Grit battled his way to the stable, fed the horses and the chickens and pigs, milked the cows, and gave half the milk to the calves to save another trip down from the house. Yaller and Sam he drove into a shed and carried hay to fill their manger. The tumbled hay in the spare stall of the stable showed him where Banty had slept, and the black shoat coming out for its breakfast told him how close had been his guess as to Banty's bedfellow. But he was too utterly weary to do more than grunt a half-finished sentence of disparagement.

He tottered when he reached the snow-piled doorstep. Once inside the cabin, his numbed fingers struggled with the buttons of his coat. He attempted to sweep the snow off his overshoes before it melted, but found it too great a task. The process of removing the overshoes stopped when he had fumbled one buckle out of its fastening. He dragged himself to his bunk, turned back two heavy blankets, and lay down, pulling them over his shoulders with his stiff, groping fingers. After that he lay for hours without moving so much as a foot.

About noon Banty awoke from a more or less troubled sleep, saw Grit lying on the opposite bunk, and called to him for whiskey. But Grit neither moved nor answered, so presently Banty heaved himself off the bunk and began rummaging the cabin for the jugs he firmly believed Grit had hidden. Under Grit's bunk, in Grit's battered trunk, in the corner where their supplies were stored, even in his own bunk and beneath it Banty searched craftily, with a dogged persistence worthy of a better object. Failing to find in the cabin what he sought, Banty wriggled himself painfully into his overcoat, put on his high Arctic overshoes and cap and mittens, and plowed through the drifts to the stable, there to continue the search.

The keen cold of the wind, at first breathtaking and hard to face, stung his sluggish energies to a point where he observed other things than possible hiding places for two willow-woven demijohns. His saddle, for instance; he did not remember taking it off Sam and hanging it on its accustomed peg just inside the stable door alongside Grit's saddle — yet there it hung with the gunny sack of tobacco and baking soda, and the bundle of newspapers still tied behind the cantle. Banty stood looking at it stupidly, forgetting his quest while he wondered how the saddle had come to be there, instead of on Sam's back.

"Grit, he was drunk las' night," he muttered. "Roarin', ravin' drunk. He's drunk today . . . plumb laid out. And anyway he'd let ole Sammy stan' fer a month with the saddle on before he'd take it off. Grit, he always did hate Sam . . . just 'cause he's mine, I guess. And I never done it. . . ."

He turned away, shaking his head in tacit dismissal of the puzzle. He looked in the cows' mangers, tossing the hay to one end, pushing the cows out of his way while he searched. Then, abruptly as a new thought struck him, he stood and looked at Liney placidly chewing her cud, uninterested in the hay.

"By gollies, I shore would like to know who's been here an' done the chores an' beat it ag'in," he mused, and continued his search in the lean-to, where the work team munched contentedly, heads buried to their eyes in their manger.

In the corral, where his wanderings finally took him to the windmill, he saw that the pump had been disconnected to save the pipe from freezing. No stranger would have thought of that; no stranger would have come to the ranch without some definite errand, and, having one, would have come to the cabin and wakened the two. Banty's head was clearing sufficiently to reject the theory that the animals had been cared for by some good-natured neighbor. Grit must have done it, and yet — "Grit shore is drunk, an', when the kid's drunk, he don't give a damn fer nothin'. An' it must 'a' been him . . . an' how do yuh figure that out?"

Lines of footprints he saw, packed full of snow, yet distinct in the untrodden expanse. With some vague hope that they might lead him to the jugs, Banty set out to follow where they led. Straight down along the corral, around the corner, on around the hay corral, in among the drifts that had formed where the loose hay piles caught and held the snow, circling the one remaining stack and out again, he followed them doggedly. On around the stable, angling away to where a fence of barbed wire blocked the way. Up the fence to the place where a high bank barred further progress, returning to the stable, retreating again to the high bank, paralleling the other lines of footprints crudely, yet never crossing them, blobbing out in the drifts where the snow was broken in lumps and there were marks of a shovel, pausing in great trampled areas wherever a clump of sage or buckbrush stood. Banty kept stubbornly on the track, wallowing through drifts that had grown higher, searching the spots swept bare of snow.

Once, on the sheltered side of the boulder that had held moisture in the ground to nourish a lone clump of willows, Banty studied a round imprint the size of a saucer. "Lantern," he read the sign briefly, and looked at the mark of a shovel set down alongside a snow-covered hummock.

"By gollies, the kid must 'a' been crazy to come away out here huntin' them." There a small doubt crept in. Was it the jugs Grit had been hunting? Banty turned with his back to the storm and gazed at the vague outline of the cabin 100 yards away. He was breathing heavily, healthily tired from his wading through the snow. The tracks went on and on, zigzagging back and forth, purposefully covering the wide space from cutbank to pasture fence. It would take him another full hour to trace them as they wove here and there, from hummock to brush, from high drift to snow-filled ditch.

From somewhere in the distance, in one of those lulls that come when a storm wind pauses to gather breath for a fresh burst of fury, he heard the faint, insistent bellowing of cattle voicing the misery they could not ease, their fear of the ultimate that they could not escape.

"Down in the willers," said Banty. "They've got to be fed, or we'll lose half of 'em."

With his breath steaming out before him,

his shoulders packed with snow, Banty toiled to the cabin. Grit lay breathing noisily, rapidly, his eyes half open and glassy, his weathered lips parted and dry. Banty stood over him, cocking one eye disapprovingly, his piratical mustache, twitching with the wordless movement of his lips.

"Drunk . . . drunker than when I left him," he was saying to himself, trying to still a fear that plucked naggingly at his reason. Quite involuntarily he leaned and held his face close to Grit's face, sniffing. Abruptly he stood up, glancing here and there around the cabin, his eyes seeking something that his startled wits could not name. Grit, he had suddenly discovered, was not drunk. His breath carried no taint of liquor, but instead the fetid odor of fever burning high and hot.

As though he would call for help — where help would never come for his calling — Banty went to the door, jerked it open, and looked out. The mournful lowing of the young cattle huddled among the willows down in the creek pasture droned through the blizzard. His eye lighted upon the blunt nose of the go-devil protruding from a drift a few feet from the door. Against one section of peeled pole, the neck of a half pint flask showed an inch or so of clear glass.

Banty looked, looked again, wondered what the go-devil was doing at the cabin, remembered dimly the jolt and the lurch of its stopping there, recalled his struggle to get up. He stared out through the snow whirl to where the gate to the creek pasture showed, blurred and indistinct, in the storm. Quite clearly now he remembered falling with that gate, his effort to get up, falling again. The gate was up and fastened securely. The go-devil was at the cabin. The stock was fed — and out there in the snow, weaving back and forth methodically, were the tracks of a man — a man who carried a lantern and a shovel in the storm.

"By gollies," whispered Banty, and closed the door softly, as though he feared to disturb Grit, whose breathing sounded loudly and raucously in the cabin. With trembling haste Banty started a fire, heated water, and folded the cleanest dishtowel he could find to make a compress. Steaming hot, passing it hurriedly from one hand to the other to escape being burned, he carried it to the bunk, pulled open Grit's shirt, and covered his chest with the towel, tucking the corners well down. The next cleanest towel he wrung out of cold water and placed on Grit's beating temples. A trickle of water meandered down Grit's stubborn jaw to his neck, but Banty did not notice and Grit did not know.

"That's jest to keep yuh ridin' easy while I git down to business. Keep yore feet hot an' yore head cold . . . I've brung 'em through a heap worse off than what you be, kid . . . by gollies, yes! Time ole Pete Larrigan fell in the Snake an' you pulled him out an' the both of yuh tuk cold . . . Pete, he dang' near cashed in that there time. He would 'a', if I hadn't 'a' got right after him with roast onion poultices an' a good sweat. Our onions is froze, but I'll fry some up in hen grease an' slap 'er on hot as you kin stand. If I jest had some good whiskey to make yuh a hot toddy an' git yuh sweatin' good. . . ."

He slanted his one-eyed gaze at Grit, watched closely for some sign that he had heard. But Grit made no movement, did not flicker an eyelid. "Well, mebby ginger'll do, in a pinch," Banty compromised, fighting back his alarm at Grit's condition, and began slicing frozen onions into a frying pan.

Then Banty went out in the keen sweep of the blizzard and mumbled his thoughts aloud, as lonely men do. Partly to dull his anxiety for Grit he talked, partly to dull that remorse that follows close on the heels of a drunken bout. What Grit had done for him he knew now as well as though he had seen it all. How Grit had come by his sickness Banty knew, also — and he knew too well how desperately ill Grit was.

He harnessed the work team and hitched them to the hay wagon, and left them standing while he plowed to the cabin to see if Grit was all right. Grit's eyes were closed; his forehead seemed less hot to Banty's cold fingers. So Banty took heart and hauled hay to the cattle, shoveling through drifts where the horses could not pull the wagon.

The cattle came crowding hungrily around the wagon — what cattle had not penetrated too deeply into the thickets to see and hear him as he passed. It was hard work, for the team edged always away from the wind and seemed never to see a drift until they were belly deep and had to stop. Whereupon Banty would wind the lines around the front stake of the rack, climb stiffly down with the shovel, and clear a way to the ten-inch level of snow through which the wagon would go squealing to the next drift.

His side was sore, and with every lift of the fork or shovel a nagging, sharp pain would win a grunt from him. Once a horse had lifted its heels unexpectedly and caught Banty in the side, and had broken two ribs.

Banty thought of that horse now, and wondered if he again possessed two broken ribs.

As a matter of fact, Grit had broken only one of Banty's ribs. But it was rather a nasty break, with a splinter of bone that was doing some damage to Banty's interior, enough to keep Banty unhappily aware of his injury. And pitching hay was not exactly the treatment a doctor would have prescribed for the hurt.

That night Banty sat by the cook stove, keeping the cabin warm and listening to Grit, who talked incessantly. Listening to Grit was not pleasant. He was reliving aloud his search for Banty, his labor in getting Banty to the cabin, his worry over the heifer that had blackleg, his anxiety over Banty's continued absence in town. Back and forth through the warp of his narrowed existence wove the shuttle of Grit's fevered thoughts. The ranch, the cattle, the weather, and Banty — always Banty! His welfare, his faults, his petty injustices, and his loyalty that was beyond all doubt.

"He's left it alone for seven months now," Grit continued. "He wouldn't slip up . . . that's why I sent him, instead of going myself. He's got to feel a feller trusts him.

We're getting ahead, now he's quit drinkin'. . . ." And he would mutter meaningless words in his queer, croaking voice.

Banty would heat the onion poultice again, and, while it was heating, he would smear Grit's chest with turpentine and lard, another one of Banty's cure-alls. Grit would open his eyes and stare wildly up into Banty's face, and talk and mutter. And Banty, his side on fire with pain, would shuffle back to the stove and sit with tears running down his cheeks, and blubber promises to Grit, who did not hear, and call himself names that he in no wise deserved.

At daylight Banty roused from a stupor that he mistook for sleep, and yelled with the pain when he stooped to reach a stick of wood for the fire. He sat blinking at the frosted window for a space, breathing shortly, trying to hope that in a minute or two the stitch would leave him and he would be able to move comfortably.

A groan from the bunk recalled more fully the horror of the night before, and he made shift to get upon his feet and somehow to reach Grit — who looked up at him sanely, plucked at his chest, and managed a rasping whisper. Banty, his teeth set in his lower lip lest he give evidence of his own plight, caught the word "doctor".

"Shore," he said, and would trust himself to say no more.

"How's . . . stock . . . makin'?"

"Fine," blurted Banty between his teeth, and turned away before Grit's wandering gaze could rest too keenly upon his face.

A doctor — sure, a doctor! They both needed a doctor, if Banty knew anything. He shuffled to the door, each sliding step a fresh agony, looked out. The wind blew bleakly across the snow, sending white clouds of it breast high, whipping it into eddies and whirling it away in an endless dance.

"I'd ruther have snow fallin' than blowin'," muttered Banty. "She's cold, she's *dang'* cold! I dunno's I kin make it in fifteen mile, guess mebby I better take Yaller. Sam, he's all right, but. . . ."

From the bunk Grit whispered echo to Banty's thought. "Better . . . ride . . . Yaller . . . ," panted Grit.

"Shore," gasped Banty, and stared hard at Grit, wondering if Grit could live while a man rode fifteen miles slowly, plodding through drifts, or while another man rode more swiftly back over those fifteen miles. He did not know whether the man who rode in could live through fifteen miles of cold.

"Only one way to find out," he told himself grimly. "That's by tryin'."

Hungry cattle followed him hopefully to where he left the creek bottom and rode up the rim rock trail to the level where the wind blew terrifically with nothing to stop it for eighty miles or so. Down that trail Banty had ridden singing, just two days ago. He was not singing now. He scarcely knew that he rode.

Once on the trail to town, Yaller plodded faithfully along, blinking into the wind, shaking the snow out of his ears when they were packed too full. When Banty would seem about to topple off, Yaller would ease his steps until his load balanced itself again. He much preferred to carry Grit, who was light and who knew how to ride. Yaller did not think much of Banty that day.

Nevertheless, he carried him into town and up to the hitching rail where Grit always stopped. When Banty neither urged him on nor dismounted, Yaller turned his head and eyed his rider curiously. Then a man came out and started down the steps, glanced at Banty and Yaller, glanced again, turned back, and spoke to someone inside. Two other men came out and joined the first.

"He ain't drunk," diagnosed the store-keeper, and shifted his quid of tobacco to the other cheek. "He was drunk when he left town day befo' yes'day, but he ain't drunk now."

"He ain't froze," stated a cowpuncher who had helped carry Banty in. "He's hot. Better hunt up Doc . . . if yuh ask me, he's sick."

"That there's Grit's horse he rode in," added another cowpuncher, and pinched out the fire on a half-smoked cigarette. "I'll go put him up. Looks queer to me . . . Banty ridin' ole Yaller. I've got a hunch something's wrong out there. I think I'll just fan out that way. Bill, you can tell the boss. . . ."

"Here's a letter," announced the store-keeper, who had been fumbling in Banty's pockets and who, being postmaster as well, assumed certain professional privileges. "It's addressed 'To the Man That Finds Me' . . . and seein' I'm postmaster here. . . ."

"Seein' you're postmaster, just hand me my mail," spoke up the cowpuncher who had started out to take care of Yaller. "I'm the man that found him."

"That's right, Bob, she's your letter," abetted Bill. Wherefore, having two against him, the postmaster surrendered Banty's note

and retired behind his barricade of pigeon-
holes.

Bob turned the envelope over twice, tore off one end, and read aloud: "Git the doctor out to Grit hes got numonia bad and a man to feed the stock they need to lodes of hay ontill the storm brakes. When the doc gits back tell him to take a look at my sid a horse kicked me and its in bad shape but not befor Grit is took care off hes awful sick so hurry out as hes alone and bad off. Yours Truley, William Grimes or Banty."

Bill was on his way for the doctor before Bob had finished reading. Bob was on his way to Grit before the doctor had buttoned himself into his fur coat — and the doctor was not a slow man.

Fortunately the doctor did not rush at once to his pneumonia patient fifteen miles away, urgent as he knew the case must be. He went first to the store, and from there he went to a telephone and dictated a wire to Pocatello. Even then he did not start for the ranch, but spent a half hour with Banty, and seemed to want to spend a much longer time with him. But at last he reached for his moleskin cap and began rebuttoning his coat for the ride before him.

"If I knew the condition of the other man . . . it's doubtful if this one pulls through. If they get him to the hospital in time . . . what? Oh, merely the threat of a very serious complication . . . you fellows call it blood poisoning."

Still he lingered, staring down at Banty, chewing a corner of his lower lip worriedly. "By God, he's game!" he said abruptly, looking up suddenly into the grave, understanding eyes of the cowpuncher, Bill. "He must have suffered hell for the last twelve hours. How he ever rode fifteen miles in his condition amazes me. I wouldn't have believed it possible."

"I would," said Bill laconically. "Grit would 'a' rode it for him, if the play come that way. Him and Grit, they'd go through hell and back for each other and think nothin' of it . . . but you might not realize it, hearin' 'em bawl each other out sometimes. You'd best not tell Grit how bad off Banty is, Doc. It'd be a heap more merciful to shoot the top of Grit's head off."

Grit and Banty do not often refer to that particular episode in their lives. A full month the cowpuncher, Bob, gathered the eggs and shut up the chickens and fed the calves and made butter and cooked and told Grit funny stories, and forked hay to the young stuff in the creek pasture when he thought they needed it, and plowed the garden — although a cowpuncher hates plowing as badly as a married man hates to cook his own meals.

They do not often refer to that month, save in the most general way. Banty knows that he is to blame for Grit's sickness. Grit knows what horse it was that kicked Banty that night with what shaved close-to-fatal effect. They know, but they never have admitted to each other that they know.

The closest they ever came to such confession was when they rode together through the creek pasture one day in early summer. Side-by-side, their stirrups clicking together now and then when Sam and Yaller stepped close, they came up the trail through the sandy wasteland where floods long past had gullied the loose soil. Banty was humming under his breath an old range tune: "Fer I'm a young cowboy, and I know I done wrong."

Grit was not doing anything much but ride and be glad in a vague, wordless way, that they two were there, and that the sun was shining and the meadowlarks were busy — glad that they were alive.

Fifty yards from the trail they had gone, and swung to the right to pass a tufted hummock crowned with a lone sagebrush. Keen-eyed, both of them, seeing everything at a glance, they saw — and looked to each other quickly, and looked away. A dark flush mounted slowly up Banty's face to his old gray hat. Grit's lips twitched at the corners, but not with smiling.

Banty turned to Grit with a queer, shamed look in his eyes, with the flush still on his face. "Booze shore kin put the devil into a man," he said. "By gollies, yes! It shore plays hell all around."

"Shore does," assented Grit, with a quick side glance at Banty.

Banty hesitated, reined back. "By gollies, they's some that won't harm nobody," he asserted under his breath, and pulled his old .45 that he carried for coyotes, and took careful aim.

One willow-woven demijohn he shot clean in its middle, whereupon Sam decided that he could remember certain fancy steps that he had practiced in his youth when six-guns popped in Shoshone and cowboys *yip-yip-yipped* their advent into town. Banty pulled him up, swearing because the abruptness of Sam's gait found the weak spot in his side, took aim again, and caused the other demijohn to become as the first — a lop-sided thing of twisted willow withes, wet and smelling strongly of whiskey.

"Got 'em both," he gloated, merely to hide the things he would not say. "I kin shoot yet with the best of 'em."

"You dang' fool, you can take yourself to another bed in the hospital, too! If I owned a horse like that Sam, I'd brain him and put him out of his misery. Tryin' to buck . . . at his age!"

"By gollies, that there's more'n what ole Yaller kin do. He can't even *try*," Banty retorted.

They rode on, *click-clack*ing over the loose rocks. In Grit's shrewd eyes was a softer light. Banty hummed contentedly his old range song:

"Fer I'm a young cowboy, and I know I done wrong."

# ABOUT THE AUTHOR

**Bertha Muzzy Bower,** born in Cleveland, Minnesota, was the first woman to make a career of writing Western fiction and remains one of the most widely known. She became familiar with cowboys and ranch life at eighteen when her family moved to Great Falls, Montana in 1889. She was nearly thirty and a mother of three before she began writing. Her first novel, *Chip of the Flying U,* was initially published as a magazine story in 1904, and was an immediate success. Bower went on to write thirteen more books about the Flying U. In 1933 she turned to stories set prior to the events described in *Chip of the Flying U. The Whoop-Up Trail* begins a trilogy recounting Chip Bennett's arrival in Montana and early adventures at the Flying U. Much of the appeal of Flying U saga is due to Bower's use of humor, the strong sense of loyalty and family depicted among her characters, as well as the authentic quality of her cowboys. She herself was a maverick who experimented with the Western story, introducing modern technologies and raising unusual social concerns — such as aeroplanes in *Skyrider* or divorce in *Lonesome Land.* She was sensitive to the lives of women on the frontier and created some extraordinary female characters, notably in Vada Williams in *The Haunted Hills,* Georgie Howard in *Good Indian,* Helen in *The Bellehelen Mine,* and Mary Allison in *Trouble Rides the Wind,* another early Chip Bennett story.

# ABOUT THE EDITOR

**Kate Baird Anderson** is an artist, writer and voracious reader with many interests, from history, etymology and archeology to needlework, gardening, and the black hole of genealogy. She is currently working on B. M. Bower's biography and Western novel reprints, and editing Bower's short stories, as well as those of grandfather Bertrand W. Sinclair, a noted Canadian author in the 1920s. Kate was born in Los Angeles County in 1929, spent much of her childhood with grandmother Bower, and has also lived in Oregon, Montana, Oklahoma, Arkansas, Indiana, and northern Illinois.

The employees of Thorndike Press hope you have enjoyed this Large Print book. All our Thorndike, Wheeler, and Kennebec Large Print titles are designed for easy reading, and all our books are made to last. Other Thorndike Press Large Print books are available at your library, through selected bookstores, or directly from us.

For information about titles, please call:
  (800) 223-1244

or visit our Web site at:
  http://gale.cengage.com/thorndike

To share your comments, please write:
  Publisher
  Thorndike Press
  10 Water St., Suite 310
  Waterville, ME 04901